MISUNDERSTOOD IN MERRITT

ALICIA HUNTER PACE

For my Family

MISUNDERSTOOD IN MERRITT

MISUNDERSTOOD IN MERRITT
Alicia Hunter Pace

CHAPTER 1

Cute got him every single time.

Sammy Anderson had no truck with tall women who were all hipbones and cheekbones and looked that they could slice a man in two just by bumping into him. In fact, they scared him with their black clingy dresses, tall shoes, big chunky jewelry, and sunglasses pushed on top of their heads like bug eyes.

But cute. He loved him some cute, and the cutest thing in Cute City had just opened the door to Annelle Mead Interiors in Merritt, Alabama, where he'd been sent to fetch house trappings for Neyland Beauford.

Fetching was what Sammy did—mostly for country music star Jackson Beauford, but really for any Beauford, because the Beaufords were all one big machine. What a lot people wouldn't have guessed was that Sammy was at the top of the list of people who kept that machine oiled and in good working condition. But the Beaufords knew, and they paid him well and treated him like family. As far as he was concerned, he had the best job in the world. The job came with many, many fringe benefits, but so far none as good as being allowed to cast his eyes on the cute, smiling girl standing in front of him. He tried his best not to think improper thoughts about her; she was probably someone's wife and mother. He let his eyes drop to her left hand. Ringless and no ridge where a ring had been.

So it wouldn't hurt to look, as long as he didn't touch.

Her soft, light red hair brushed her shoulders and was smooth and feathery all at once. It was his favorite kind of hair, though he hadn't known it until that moment. Technically, having not touched it, he couldn't be absolutely sure it was soft, but he was sure enough—and enough served him well. It always had. Swear to Thor's thunder, her big, round eyes were an amazing shade of emerald green. There was a sprinkling of freckles on her nose and across her round little cheeks. He would have loved to run his thumb over her bare suggestion of a double chin, but that wasn't allowed. You couldn't just go around touching people you'd never even spoken to.

"Hey. I'm Sammy Anderson."

Though she rewarded him for introducing himself by widening her smile, he still shouldn't touch her face—let alone her curvy, little body. He figured she wasn't quite five and a half feet tall, and her body had been built for cuddling and wearing an apron—maybe at the same time, maybe not. Not that there needed to be any cooking involved in the apron-wearing. He could cook. He just needed her to wear an apron because she would look even cuter. She wasn't wearing one now, of course, and he could think of no better pastime than picking her up, sitting down on that fancy couch across the way, and settling her on his lap. Parts in his lap region liked that idea, but he was pretty sure that couch was just as off limits to him as she was.

"I'm Pam Carson," she said. "I work for Lucy and Annelle." Lucy Kincaid was always driving up to Beauford Bend to help Jackson's wife, Emory, pick out paint colors and curtains. Now Jackson's brother Gabe and his wife had bought a new house, and Lucy was doing the same for them.

So Pam worked for Lucy, like he worked for the Beaufords. That was common ground—sort of.

She stepped aside to let him in. She wore a green, full skirt that hit right above her knees and a sweater that was a little too loose and a little too long. He would bet she wouldn't wear a sweater that fit because she thought she was fat. He never ceased to be amazed at the women who thought they were fat just because they couldn't saw you in two with their body parts.

He gave her his best smile. "I'm here to pick up some stuff? A rug and some pictures?" There was another woman sitting on a stool behind the counter. He glanced at her, but she just didn't sink into his soul the way Pam did.

He scrubbed at the mustard stain on the front of his shirt, as if that would make it go away, as if that would make Pam say, "Forget the pictures and rug, Sammy. Let's go sit on that couch and cuddle. But first, let me get my apron."

Ha! As if. He'd gotten that mustard stain when he'd detoured though Decatur, Alabama—like he did every time he got the chance—to eat C.F. Penn's hamburgers, which he considered to be the best on the planet. Like him, the burgers were uncomplicated and ordinary. The patties were part meat but mostly bread, fried crisp and sandwiched between soft, white buns that had no seeds and no wholegrain foolishness. When you walked in, a waitress behind the counter asked, "All the way?" which meant bright yellow mustard and lots of raw onion. If you wanted ketchup and cayenne pepper, you added it yourself, but Sammy never did. "All the way" in its purest state was good enough for him, and he always ate three, never wasting any stomach space on french fries. Salad wasn't even an option.

Gwen, the catering manager for Around the Bend, Emory Beauford's party business, would not have approved, and Sammy ought to know. Every week, he spent countless hours carting her around in one of the Around the Bend vans so she could sniff melons, squeeze peaches, taste cheese, and interrogate farmers about the chemicals they used and the living conditions of their chickens and dairy cows.

No doubt if the mustard on his shirt had come from Gwen, it would have been brown with seeds in it, and she would have made it herself. But in the end, he would have still slopped on his shirt. Like everyone at Beauford Bend, Sammy loved Gwen. He even appreciated the fine food she put on the table. But he couldn't help but wonder if some of the people at the parties Emory put on wouldn't like a Penn's burger instead of goat cheese crème brûlée and cornbread muffins stuffed with raw salmon.

He eyed Pam again. He wondered if she would eat Penn's hamburgers with him.

"Right back here." She began to walk away from him. Back there? Oh, right. For a second he thought she meant there were hamburgers back there. He fell in step behind her.

"Hey," he said to the woman sitting on the stool behind the counter.

Pam led him through a door to a storeroom filled with furniture and boxes.

"Here." She stopped and pointed to a stack of boxes. "These are little antique silver pieces. Not breakable, though they are wrapped well. And this is the artwork." There were three flat crates—one large and two smaller.

"Looks manageable."

"The rug might not be quite as easy."

When she bent down and put her hand on the large plastic-wrapped roll, her too loose sweater gaped.

Thor's thunder.

He shouldn't look, but he did. Any fool would have. He hadn't been able to tell anything about her breasts before, but now he could. And she had no idea he was looking.

"This is an antique silk Persian carpet." She sounded so serious.

He nodded. "Persia. Yeah." Her breasts were lush globes encased in white lace. He was pretty sure they would fit perfectly in his hands.

"We wrapped it in acid free paper, with muslin on top of that."

"Double wrap. Probably a good idea." Was he a peeping Tom since she didn't know he could see? Not that he could see all that well—not nearly well enough, anyway. Not a nipple in sight.

"Really, triple wrapped with the plastic on the outside." He looked away from more interesting things to meet her green eyes—*serious* green eyes. She meant business about that rug. Had he not been able to see her nipples because of the angle? Or maybe they just were not at attention. He could take care of that, could just imagine them coming to life against his fingertips—just like his nether regions were coming to life right now.

He nodded like he cared about rug wrappings. "Yes. I see. The plastic is probably smart."

She shook her head. "It isn't good for the rug. It's only there for transporting. I understand the rug is to be put in place tonight, but if that changes, please remove the plastic."

"I can do that." He could remove her bra, too. First he'd cuddle her on the forbidden couch, and then he'd remove her bra.

"Good." She started to rise, but lost her balance a little.

Sammy was nothing if not a man of action. If he had one talent, it was anticipating the needs of others, and Pam needed not to fall. He caught her hand and steadied her.

People talked about lightning striking and electric shocks, but he didn't feel that when he touched her. It was more like ripples of warm water that drifted from his head throughout his body, causing his stomach to turn over and his groin to throb.

She blushed, so maybe she felt it, too. "Sorry. Clumsy. Always have been."

"No, you're not." He didn't let go of her hand. They looked at each other for a second and smiled a connecting kind of smile. Unless he missed his guess, she liked what she saw when she looked at him, too. She looked like she wanted him to kiss her—almost as much as he wanted to kiss her.

He was going to do it, too. Nothing could stop him. But he was just inclining his face toward her when something *did* stop him.

Onions. Three hamburgers' worth. And not those sweet Vidalias that Gwen was partial to. Plain old, strong, make-you-cry-when-you-chop-them onions, onions that did not pave the way to a kiss.

He dropped her hand. "I guess I'll get the rug first."

Damn onions. Damn Penn's hamburgers. Though it was just as well. He needed to get out of here right damn now. Pam Carson was way, way out of his league.

~

I'll bet there's a pinup poster of him on Olympus. That's what Pam had said to her friend, Audrey, when she'd first caught sight of Sammy though the glass door. Audrey, a former ESPN reporter, was relatively new to Merritt and had been handpicked by the head football coach, Nathan Scott, to be president of the Merritt High Football Booster Club. Pam could hardly believe they had become such good friends in such a short amount of time—and she could not believe that Audrey didn't seem to agree with Pam's assessment of Sammy's looks. He possessed everything a pinup ought to have—dark, messy hair, dimples, and cornflower blue eyes with lashes like Bambi's. And even if she didn't have a body herself to write home about, she knew a stunning one when she saw it—6'2", with biceps and a six-pack that showed through his tight T-shirt.

She had been enjoying looking at him—and that was all. Chubby girls didn't get their hopes up about men who looked like Sammy Anderson. It was all about look but don't touch. But then he'd touched her. True enough, she'd tripped and he'd caught her, but he hadn't let go right away, not until the warmth that started at the point of contact had spread throughout her body and her scalp tingled.

Then, wonder of wonders, he'd inclined his head toward her, inch by inch, until she'd known he was going to kiss her for sure, so sure that she'd raised her face and parted her lips.

And then…nothing. He'd changed his mind. Probably had caught sight of her pudgy thigh.

He'd let go of her hand. "I guess I'll get the rug first."

That's when the embarrassment had hit.

But he didn't have to know she knew that he had been going to kiss her. "I'll prop the door open for you." She ran ahead of him, propped open the front door, and retreated to her safe place behind the counter where Audrey sat eating the dinner she'd brought for them. Pam hid her chips under her napkin.

"Wouldn't it have been easier for him to back into the alley and load that stuff out the back door?" Audrey asked.

Right. And that was what Pam had intended. She'd meant to have him move his truck, but she'd been too discombobulated. Best to sound glib. Audrey didn't know he'd almost kissed her.

"It's easier to watch him from here." Pam sat on her stool.

Sammy made trip after trip from the storeroom to his truck, and each time, he had to breeze past her. She busied herself by preparing the invoice and tried not to look, but it was hard.

After loading the last box, Sammy came to stand in front of the counter. "That it?" he asked, giving his hands a soft I'm-done-here clap. He looked a little chagrined, and was probably wondering why he had ever contemplated kissing her.

"Yes. If you'll just sign." She edged the paper toward him.

When he leaned over the counter to sign, his hair fell over his forehead, and she caught his smell—soap, sweat, and was that hamburgers? Only a girl who loved hamburgers would pick up on that. It was probably her imagination anyway. After scribbling his name, he accepted the copy Pam gave him and smiled a big, white, perfect smile. "Ladies. Have a good evening."

She would have preferred to keep her seat, but she had no choice but to follow him. Someone had to lock the front door, and she couldn't very well ask Audrey to do it. She didn't work here. Pam only hoped Sammy didn't think she was following him.

He opened his truck door but paused with his foot on the running board. He gave a little wave and followed it up with a heartbreak smile, mixed in with a frown.

Pam locked the door, turned, and walked away.

Might as well. Sammy Anderson was way, way out of her league.

CHAPTER 2

June, three months later

Sammy was moving cases of champagne from the Around the Bend catering kitchen to the ballroom when he got the two-word text message from Jackson. *Music room,* it said. Jackson always did that when he summoned Sammy—just sent the location. There was no need for the time. The time was always the same: right damn now. And Sammy was okay with that, flattered that he was indispensable to Jackson. Some insisted that no one was indispensable, but Sammy knew better. It wasn't as if Jackson would dry up and die without him, but the man's life would be a lot harder. And they both knew it.

"The master calls," he said.

"Better go, then," Gwen said.

"I'll finish moving the champagne when I'm done."

"Don't worry about it," Gwen said. "Dirk and Rafe were in the kitchen making sandwiches. I'll get them to do it."

Dirk was Gwen's husband and Jackson's head of security, and Rafe Beauford was one of Jackson's twin brothers, but no one was too good to pitch in and make a party happen. That's how things worked at Beauford Bend.

The original house had been built in 1819, with additions added at different points over the years. It had been in the Beauford family all that time, and they were proud of that. During lean times, it had become run down and stripped of its fine furnishings, but Jackson had rectified that as soon as his first album went platinum when he was nineteen. They gave tours here now on certain days, and some said it had the most beautiful grounds in the country.

But for all that, to the Beaufords, it was just a house and a place for Emory to run her party business. Some wondered why the wife of one of country music's biggest and richest stars insisted giving parties for hire, but Sammy understood, as he understood most things about the Beaufords.

It was about tradition. The Beauford men's mother, Laura, and great aunt Amelia had started the business, and Miss Amelia had kept it up after the tragic fire that killed the boys' parents and little sister. Emory, who had been working in the business for a few years, took over after Miss Amelia died. That was way before she caught Jackson's eye.

Miss Amelia had hired Sammy when he was a teen, and he'd been here ever since. No one had ever said to him, "You don't really work for Around the Bend anymore. You now pander to Jackson." It had just evolved. Like everyone else on the place, he just did the work that needed doing, but pandering was his specialty. Though Lord knows he could be dense at times, Sammy had always had a bit of intuition about what people needed, sometimes when they didn't even know themselves. Over the years, he had developed that skill into a fine art.

Sammy exited the main part of the house and took the stairs to the family wing, where Jackson's state-of-the-art music room was located. He expected to find Jackson at the piano composing or plugged into a headset listening to recently laid down tracks. But no. He was sprawled on one of the big leather couches, looking exasperated.

"I need you to go to Merritt," Jackson said.

"Yeah?" Sammy let himself down on the other couch across from Jackson. He hadn't been to Merritt since that day back in March when he'd gone to pick up some house stuff for Neyland. And he'd thought about Pam Carson every single day since and Googled her more times than he should have. If he'd thought she was out of his league the day he met her, the Googling had brought it home for sure.

Not only did she work in that high-class shop with Lucy Kincaid, she was on some important sounding arts and culture board of directors. Her father was a stockbroker, and her mother was a former concert pianist. (His mother played piano at the Bethel Baptist Church, but that wasn't much common ground.) Pam's brother was some kind of computer guy who'd invented a game that it seemed like Sammy was supposed to know about but didn't. Before that, the brother had been on the USA Olympic swim team. He hadn't won anything, but still. (Sammy could swim and use a computer. Again, not much common ground.) Pam's sister was a micro-biologist married to another microbiologist. Together, they had done something great, though Sammy didn't understand one thing about it. (So, no common ground.)

Pam still lived with her parents, so Sammy—thanks to his good friend, Google, again— had been able to see a street view of where she lived. The house was no Beauford Bend, but it was a far cry from the rancher he'd grown up in or the renovated carriage house where he lived at Beauford Bend.

"… can't turn Missy loose with this." Jackson brought him back to the present. "Sammy, are you listening to me?"

"Always," Sammy said sincerely. "I live to listen to you." And he had been, sort of. This had something to do with Jackson's cousin, Missy Bragg, and how she couldn't be trusted with something—probably something to do with the benefit concert Missy had talked Jackson into doing in Merritt at the end of the month. Dread washed over Sammy. Missy was a nice woman, but she was a force of nature. There wasn't much Sammy couldn't handle, but he knew his limitations, and Missy was one of them.

Jackson looked doubtful. "I'm going to repeat myself just in case you didn't get it all."

Sammy took out the small notebook he kept in his back pocket for such occasions. "Go."

"Okay. I'm doing a concert to benefit the Arts and Cultur Center in Merritt." That was the same board Pam served on. Best not think about that.

"I know all that." Sammy wrote it down anyway, along with the date—June 30.

"The concert is small—they are only selling a thousand tickets." That was incredibly small for a Jackson Beauford concert. "But it's on a farm somewhere, and they're having barbecue and beer, which Missy, no doubt, got for free from somebody. People tell her yes so she will shut her mouth."

"Is that why you told her yes so close to your own benefit concert?" That would be for the Vanderbilt Burn Center on July Fourth weekend.

Jackson shrugged. "She's family. Plus, Will Garrett is an avid supporter of the center, and I owe him." Will was a master woodworker—famous, Sammy had been told. He'd taken the youngest Beauford brother as an apprentice after Beau had gotten hurt in the army and had to come home. And if family was the moon and stars to Jackson, baby brother Beau was the sun and the whole universe.

"Anyway, the concert comes at the end of that high school football camp that Missy is co-chairing—the one that Gabe is helping with." Gabe played for the Tennessee Titans and was Rafe's twin. "All of this is for that arts center."

"So why exactly do I need to go to Merritt?"

Jackson closed his eyes and shook his head. "When Missy gets it in her mind to raise money for something, she raises a lot of money—which means she wants to spend none. So she had Brantley Kincaid draw up plans for a stage and has been rounding up local volunteers and high school football players to build the thing."

"No." Sammy shook his head. "Can't happen." Jackson usually performed in arenas, but the kind of show he put on required a stage with all kinds of bells and whistles—and it had to be built by someone who knew what they were doing.

"You got that right. Not unless I'm going to appear with no band, no equipment, and no crew. What she's got in mind would just about support one man, a stool, and a guitar. God help us if a dog were to run on stage."

"Why didn't she just get you a flatbed truck?"

"That would probably be safer. Brantley called me and told me all this. He's a good architect, and he knows this has no business happening."

"Then why did Brantley agree?"

Jackson raised his hands. "Why does anybody agree to do what Missy says? So in the end, she's getting what she wants—a stage that costs her nothing. I hired a company out of Colorado. We haven't used them, but lots of big names have. I need you to go to Merritt and supervise. This outfit knows what they are doing, but I've got to have somebody there, and I don't trust anyone else to do this but you."

Sammy still took pleasure in that. He and Jackson had gotten off to a rocky start when they'd first met, but that was all just a bad memory. If Jackson said a thing, it was true.

"When would I go? How long would I stay?"

"Tuesday, as in tomorrow. The stage people aren't coming until next week, but I'd feel better if you could get a look at the venue and make sure everything that needs to be done in advance is done."

And that would be plenty. It always was.

"And I'd like you to stay until after the concert is over, the stage is disassembled, and that farm is cleaned up. Other things are bound to come up."

Sammy scratched his head. "I'll go. I've never told you no. But handling Missy…"

"You won't really have to. Now that everything is planned, she has put somebody else in charge of the concert and barbecue. She's going to concentrate on the football camp, which is really the main event. Though I should mention Missy has offered to let you stay in her pool house. The only hotel in Merritt is going to be full of football players. I can insist on her finding you somewhere else, but Missy's got a really nice pool house, and she will feed you well."

"The pool house is fine." He'd stayed in worse places doing Jackson's bidding. Maybe Missy would leave his food outside the door.

"I really appreciate this, Sammy. There will be a nice bonus for you."

There always was. Jackson took care of his own. "So who's building this stage? I'll need to check in with them."

"Yeah." Jackson reached for his phone and began to scroll though. "The name of the company is Mile High Stages. I've got the contact information. Here it is. I'll text it to you. I told them to do what you say."

Great. Jackson often told third parties that, and they always *loved* it.

"You'll need to know the Merritt contact, too." He scrolled through his phone. "Here. Pam Carson. I'm sending you her contact info."

Well, well, well. He hadn't seen that coming—though

maybe he should have, what with her being on that board of directors. But, while Sammy was an expert at anticipating others, he often didn't see things coming that concerned himself.

Cute, classy, out-of-his-league Pam. And he'd be seeing her, maybe every day. He didn't know whether to be happy about that or not. That often happened to him, too.

At more or less the same time

The boardroom of the Alden Fairfax Brantley Culture Center, otherwise known as the Brantley Building, Merritt, Alabama

Pam lifted her hair off the back of her neck. It was hot.

The president of the board spoke. "I hereby call this meeting of the Arts and Cultural Board to order." Tiptoe Watkins wasn't usually so formal, but you could never tell about him. He was a Harvard-educated cemetery owner who tuned pianos on the side. If that didn't equal eccentricity, nothing did. "We'll try not to drag this out. I probably should have relocated the meeting."

"I do apologize," town matriarch Caroline Brantley said, as if it were her fault the air conditioning was on the fritz. She was the widow of Judge Alden Fairfax Brantley and had donated the building to the city, so she must have felt some measure of responsibility. "Apparently the air conditioning unit went out last night. My grandson discovered it when he came back to his office to get something. He contacted Bennett, and they called the repairman." Brantley Kincaid had his architectural offices in the building.

The center director, Bennett Watkins, did not let the heat stop him from eating doughnuts and chasing them with hot coffee. "It should be fixed in time for Children's Art Camp this afternoon."

"Why don't we just get a report on Fifth Quarter and reconvene next week for the regular business?" Byron Masters suggested. Fifth Quarter was shorthand for Fifth Quarter: All-Stars for Art, the upcoming fundraiser they were doing in conjunction with the high school football team to enable them to fund an art therapy program. Pam had known that name was too long when the co-chairs, Miss Caroline and Missy Bragg, came up with it, but Pam didn't have the gumption to state dissenting opinions to many people, let alone those two. It's not that they weren't nice—just the opposite in fact. But they were so capable and sure of themselves. How did people get there?

Audrey Evans fanned herself with a file folder, and her new engagement ring sparkled in the sunlight. She absentmindedly twisted her hair onto the back of her head and secured it with an elastic band, creating a look that could have been done in an upscale salon. Maybe if Audrey decided she didn't like being a sports photographer, she could become a hair stylist. That would be handy for Pam. She wouldn't have to go to the salon. But she could only imagine what her mother—the biggest snob on the planet—would have to say about Pam's best friend having such a lowly profession, though not so lowly as Pam's "shop girl" job.

"I agree with Byron," Audrey said. "Let's reconvene next week. That is, if there's nothing pressing."

Tiptoe nodded. "Excellent idea. I'll just turn the meeting over to Caroline and Missy then." Missy was not a member of the board, but was in attendance as co-chair of Fifth Quarter.

"We'll be as brief as possible," Miss Caroline said. "Missy and I will bring you up to date on the camp. Tolly is having a sonogram this morning so Nathan couldn't be here, but

Audrey, feel free to add anything. And then we'll let Pam fill you in on the plans for the Jackson Beauford concert and barbecue."

Yes, she had been pressed into service to handle the logistics of the event that would take place at the end of the camp, but only after the important details were set. Pam had her doubts that Missy would let go of it—which was fine with Pam.

Missy opened her laptop. "As you know, the camp begins on Saturday, with registration and orientation Friday night. We're planning a cookout at the high school for the attendees, their parents, and all the volunteers, which, of course, includes all of you."

"So everybody in town?" Tiptoe said.

"I wouldn't go so far as to say that," Missy said. "But we are planning for a few hundred. The Rotary is going to grill hamburgers and hotdogs, and the Junior League is doing desserts and drinks. Between corporate sponsorship and donations, I don't think we will have to buy anything."

"Missy has done a wonderful job with securing backing," Miss Caroline said. "It's our goal for all the money we take in from the attendees to be pure profit."

"How many spaces do we have left to fill for the camp?" Byron asked.

Missy smiled like the Cheshire cat. "That's the best news. None. And we've got a waiting list. There isn't another bed to be had at the Merritt Inn."

Applause broke out.

"It's no wonder," Audrey said. "Missy and Nathan have some really big name pro players and college scouts coming. This is a great opportunity for these boys."

Missy laughed. "It helps when you have a cousin who has two Super Bowl rings and has played for two pro teams. He has managed to talk a few Tennessee Titans and San Antonio Wranglers into spending a little time with us."

"Sounds like everything is going well," Tiptoe said. "Those Beauford boys sure are being good to us, what with Gabe helping with the camp and Jackson doing the concert."

"Which brings us to the concert. Pam." Missy inclined her head toward Pam like a benevolent queen.

Pam opened her folder. "Missy has done most of the work on this so far. The camp ends on Friday, and the concert will be that night at Luke and Lanie Avery's farm. Depot Barbecue is donating the food, and Good Times Rentals is providing tables, chairs, and portable toilets."

Missy shuddered at the mention of portable toilets. Lanie Avery was a member of Missy's posse, so there was no doubt that Lanie's private powder room would be available to Missy. There was also no doubt that Pam would be fumbling around in one of those smelly little boxes, with wet wipes and hand sanitizer in her pocket.

Pam carried on. "We limited ticket sales to a thousand, and it sold out in fifteen minutes. We also have two hundred tickets to give to corporate sponsors. The camp attendees and volunteers will get in free—though we are asking the boys to help with serving food, hauling trash, and such."

Bennett let out a low whistle. "And these tickets were how much?"

"Three hundred dollars," Pam said.

"So the concert alone could support the art therapy program for a while," Bennett said.

"That's the plan," Pam said. "There may a few unavoidable expenses for things that cannot be donated like insurance, site security, and a temporary liquor license, but it's minimal. Jackson Beauford is bringing his own equipment, personal security, and crew. The venue is free, and Brantley Kincaid designed a stage. We're recruiting volunteers to build it.

Since we plan to utilize the Beauford High team, that will have to be done before the camp starts. So if you know anyone who might be willing to help—" Pam stopped short when she caught motion out of the corner of her eye. Missy had raised her hand, palm out, and was shaking her head. And she looked, well, *embarrassed*. Was that possible?

"I'm sorry." Missy looked at the table and bit her lip. "Pam, I especially apologize to you. You, too, Miss Caroline. There has been a change of plans, and there's no excuse for not letting you know that." She looked up and met Pam's eye. Indeed, she had the look of a thwarted woman. Pam was too amazed and curious to be annoyed. "There is just so much going on, and I didn't find this out until this morning."

"It's all right," Pam said. Ha! Imagine *her* telling Missy Bragg something was all right.

Missy let out a huffy breath. "I love Jackson, and we all know how talented he is, but he's a control freak."

Pam literally bit the inside of her cheek to keep a straight face. Considering the amount of shuffling, coughing, and throat clearing going on around the table, it was apparent that everyone was having the same issue.

"I guess it's understandable that he would be paranoid after what happened at his concert in California a few years ago. Do y'all know about that? A disgruntled fan threw a fire bomb on stage, and some attendees and members of his band died."

Pam remembered it. If she had been a braver person, she would have pointed out that Jackson might know more about stage productions than they did. And she might have added that she would like to know sooner rather than later what this change of plan was. After all, she was supposed to be in charge now.

"Missy," Tiptoe said, "are you saying Jackson has decided not to do the concert?"

"Oh, no! No. Nothing like that. But I had this whole stage thing handled. It would have been fine. But Jackson won't have it. He says it's not safe and Brantley doesn't know anything about stages."

"My grandson is a wonderful architect, but Jackson might have a point," Miss Caroline said. "I don't believe Brantley has ever built a stage."

"I'm sure it would have been fine," Missy said. "But Jackson has hired some company to do it. Did you know there are people who do nothing but that? Build stages for festivals and concerts?" She didn't wait for an answer. "He talked a lot about weight bearing, electricity, lighting, and sound. Finally, I just told him fine! He's paying for it."

"Big of you," Byron deadpanned.

"Thank you, Byron." Apparently Missy didn't get deadpanning. "Anyway, these people are coming from Colorado next week to get started."

Pam's head spun and she made a decision. Either she was going to run this thing or she wasn't. And she intended to know right now. She picked up her pen. "Do Luke and Lanie know about the change in plans, and is it all right with them?"

"No," Missy said. "I haven't had time, but I'll—"

"I'll go by the candy shop and talk to Lanie when I leave here," Pam said. The air conditioning at Heavenly Confections would be working, and she just might have herself a heavenly confection or two. Definitely a chocolate star and maybe a coffee truffle.

Missy looked surprised, but nodded. "They will be fine with it."

"I'm sure they will," Pam said. "But I'll talk to them. Now, what about this company? What's the name? Do you have contact information?"

Missy smiled and relief washed over her face. "No. And

you don't have to worry about that at all. Jackson is sending one of his employees down here to deal with that. He's coming tomorrow and staying in my pool house until after the concert. You'll just need to work with him."

Pam's scalp prickled, and thoughts she'd tried to chase away moved to the forefront of her brain. Surely it wouldn't be Sammy Anderson. It couldn't be. This was an important job, one that definitely would not be done by someone who picked up rugs and artwork.

"Who?" she asked.

"Sammy Anderson," Missy said.

Audrey met her eyes and smirked, serving to remind Pam how she had gone on and on to Audrey about Sammy's outstanding looks. Pam tried to make her face say, "What? I don't know what you mean." It didn't work; Audrey gave her the "Oh, please" look. And to think she had once longed for a friend of this ilk.

Missy went on, "Sammy's Jackson's right-hand man. You'll love him. He's a sweetheart."

And that was exactly what she was afraid of.

CHAPTER 3

Though she didn't have the morning coffee habit of most, Pam made a pot as soon as she arrived at work the next morning. She hadn't slept much, and she needed caffeine. Before yesterday, she had mostly put Sammy Anderson out of her mind. After all, who hadn't admired a perfect specimen of a human being on the street? It was meaningless. As for him almost kissing her—maybe she'd been wrong. She'd stumbled. He'd caught her. It had made no difference whether she had imagined the almost kiss or not.

But now it did. He was coming to town today, and she was going to have to talk to him eventually. And who wanted to talk to a man who had changed his mind practically mid-kiss—*if* that's what had happened. She was making too much of this, but when she was embarrassed, she tended to stumble all over herself.

He probably wouldn't even remember her. Lots of people didn't. It was probably best if she just pretended it hadn't happened and refused to be embarrassed. Good luck with that.

But almost kissing Sammy—or not—wasn't all that was

on her mind. There was also this fundraiser. Damn this concert and everything that went with it—the stage, the food, people calling wanting tickets, gluten-free and vegetarian meals, and backstage passes. But most of all, damn Sammy and her lack of concentration.

She wanted nothing more than to stay hidden and alone today, but that would have been impossible even if she hadn't still been living in her parents' house. Lucy and Annelle were in Atlanta on a buying trip, leaving Pam alone in the shop until noon when Paige, who worked part time, would come in. Plus, she had a whole list of fundraiser to-dos on her plate: secure insurance for the event, call Depot Barbecue and ask if they had any gluten-free and vegetarian options, listen to Depot Barbecue laugh in her face, and find out if the portable toilets came with toilet paper and hand sanitizer. Yep. This was a glamorous job, for sure.

She ought to make those calls now, while the shop was quiet, but instead she brought up her laptop and Googled Sammy—not for the first time. She knew what she'd find and it wasn't much. Still, she searched again every so often hoping something had been added. He didn't even have the decency to have a Facebook or Instagram account. It's the least he could have done for those in the world who appreciate beauty.

There were hundreds of Sammy Andersons, but only three entries came up when she searched "Sammy Anderson and Jackson Beauford," two of which only mentioned that he was a member of Jackson's entourage. The third, however, was an interview with Emory Beauford in *Twang* magazine, done a month after the birth of Jackson and Emory's daughter. There was a lot of stuff about Jackson's brothers and how their wives were Emory's best friends and how they all lived on or near the Beauford ancestral plantation.

"I won't say that we're just a typical family. Nobody who has a

private plane can really make that claim. One day, we might fly off to the Grammys or to watch Gabe play football. But the next, we might all be pitching in make sure an Around the Bend event comes off perfectly. There are no divas at Beauford Bend—even Jackson, as much as he'd like to be sometimes. In an emergency, Jackson has been known climb into a cherry picker and replace the white lights in one of the oak trees that line the drive. Yes, we have staff, and no, we don't do everything for ourselves. But we tend to forget where family leaves off and those who make our lives easier begins. For instance, I can't cook, but luckily for us, we have Gwen Thornton. She's not only the catering manager for the business, but she also makes sure the rest of us eat. Gwen's husband, Dirk, is head of security, and they were high school friends of Jackson's. And then there's Sammy Anderson. He used to work for Around the Bend, but Jackson stole him from me. I guess if Sammy had a title it would be personal assistant to Jackson, but we don't think in those terms. We just know we couldn't do without him. We had to hire another events business when Jackson and I got married, because everyone who works at Beauford Bend was in the wedding party."

There was more, but that was the most interesting thing in the article. There were pictures, lots of pictures, all full of beautiful, thin, enchanting people. Sammy was in a few—one of him wearing a tux in the afore mentioned wedding. Appealing as that was, it wasn't nearly as endearing as the one of the family boarding an airplane, with Sammy following with a blond Beauford toddler in his arms. Pam enlarged the picture and studied it for a long time. Every time she looked at it, she hoped she was improving his looks in her imagination. But no. He fit in perfectly with all those beautiful people.

She suddenly closed the window. That picture was dangerous, and she didn't have time or inclination for danger. If she'd known a way to block herself from bringing it up again, she would have done it.

But there was no need to go to such lengths, because just then the front door opened.

"I'm tried of my bedroom," Sophie Ann McGowan said as soon as she stepped foot into the shop. "I want a change."

"Hello, Sophie Ann!" Pam must have been even more in need of a distraction than she'd realized, because she felt happy to see this woman. That had never happened to her before. If the look on Sophie Ann's face was an indicator, it had never happened to her either, and not just from Pam. From anyone. Small wonder. She seemed to think that everyone in Merritt existed to serve or entertain her.

Sophie Ann looked wide-eyed and confused, but she recovered quickly and went straight to the emerald green sofa and sat down. Consultations were easier when the clients were willing to sit at the counter in the back of the store nearer the fabric samples and paint chips, but Sophie Ann was not interested in being accommodating.

Well, no matter. It's not as if Pam would be doing the consultation anyway. Before Sophie Ann had a chance to demand it, Pam poured coffee into one of Annelle's vintage Art Deco cups and added exactly three-quarters of a pack of Stevia and a half-teaspoon of cream, like she'd done a hundred times before. Sophie Ann didn't have Pam fooled. She insisted on exactly those amounts to test people and find them lacking.

"Have you given any thought to what kind of changes you'd like to make to your bedroom?" Pam asked.

"I have. Thank you, dear." Sophie Ann accepted the coffee.

Dear. That was new. Sophie Ann wouldn't think she was so dear after she imparted the bad news. Pam sat beside her on the sofa and opened her notebook.

"Annelle and Lucy are out of the shop today, but why don't you tell me what you are thinking, and I'll pass it on.

They can get some ideas together and call you for a more extensive consultation."

Sophie Ann frowned and turned her lips inward, clearly trying to decide how she was going to react to the unforgivable sin of Lucy and Annelle's failure to be available for her unannounced visit.

Finally, she nodded. "I believe I want you to do this for me, Pam."

Oh, hell. "Me?" She'd had her own jobs before, had clients who requested her, even. But not Sophie Ann. Unlike Annelle and Lucy, Pam was not an interior designer and never would be. That required a degree and passing a test. She hadn't been a good student in high school, and her freshman—and only—year of college five years ago had been nothing short of misery, not to mention a failure. She'd gone to work in the shop shortly after and had been there ever since. Her parents, who still weren't over it, had told everyone Pam had taken a year off from college to decide if she wanted to go to design school. No doubt, they would have told everyone she was trying to decide if she wanted to be a pastry chef if she'd gotten the job at the Bake Shop.

But it turned out she had a knack with colors and furniture placement. Lucy had encouraged her to go to design school, though that was out of the question. But she was happy working for Annelle and Lucy, and she didn't consider it a dead-end job, even if her parents did. While it was true that without an interior design degree she couldn't call herself a designer, let alone hang out her own shingle, Pam just felt lucky to have worked herself into a position where she could do what she loved. As far as not being able to go to work for another design firm—what did she care? She wasn't going anywhere, anyway. Having her own shop was unthinkable, even if she did fantasize about it from time to time.

But still. This was Sophie Ann. "Are you sure you don't

want to wait for Lucy? Or Annelle?" *Say yes! Please say yes, you'll wait. I can't deal with you!* There wasn't a harder to please woman in all of Merritt—and not just in this shop. It was the same everywhere she went—the bookshop, the bakery, the candy shop. Rumor had it that she had once complained to Lou Anne that her piecrust wasn't flaky enough, and Lou Anne had chased her into the street with a frying pan. Lou Anne would neither confirm nor deny.

So this wasn't good. If Pam had a talent, other than being able to design a window treatment, she could read people, which, come to think of it, might be more of a curse. It was almost a sixth sense, and she knew the only reason Sophie Ann was allowing her to do this was because she was mad that Annelle and Lucy were not available. Pam could almost hear her thinking, "I'll show them!"

"Why not you?" Sophie Ann asked. "You did a lovely job of choosing the fabric for my dining room drapes." In truth, Pam had not chosen the fabric at all. She had merely agreed with Sophie Ann's choice. "Besides, Annelle's tastes are a little too bohemian for me." She frowned at the lotus-shaped black and gold cup in her hand.

Pam could not let that stand, regardless of the ire she might in inspire. Annelle had been good to her. "Annelle does love edgy designs, but she is very good at separating her personal tastes from those of her clients. And Lucy has always pleased you."

"Eventually. But it took her a year to find the tea service I wanted."

That was true, but not fair. Sophie Ann had wanted a sterling—not to be confused with silver plate—set with coffee, tea, and chocolate pots, a kettle on a stand with a burner, plus a waste bowl, and other accoutrements that Pam had blocked out. Lucy had actually traveled to Charleston and New Orleans looking for the thing. Eventually she'd found it, but it hadn't been easy. Pam was tempted to ask Sophie Ann if she had many tea parties, but with the way things were going, the woman might to decide to have one just for the two of them.

"I don't have a year to wait on my bedroom. I have a month," Sophie Ann said.

Pam considered pointing out that it wouldn't take Lucy a year to redo a bedroom, but who could tell? Sophie Ann might want light switch covers carved from the bones of medieval saints.

"Can *you* do it in a month?" Sophie Ann demanded.

Pam opened her notebook. "What do you have in mind? New furniture? Any structural changes?"

"No. Nothing like that. Mostly a different color scheme. You know. Paint, window treatments, bedding. New upholstery for the sofa and wing chairs. Maybe a rug and lamps."

"That shouldn't be a problem so long as the fabrics you choose are available. When do you need the work completed?"

"July 1. I'm leaving for Europe tomorrow, and I want everything done while I'm gone. And I don't want to choose fabric. I want you to do it. I don't have time, but I want a whole new look when I get back. And I don't want to come home to a mess."

That was a first. Sophie Ann was usually a micro-micro-manager. "What kind of color scheme do you have in mind?"

"I want autumnal colors. I went out to work in my flowers this morning before seven, and I got so hot that I began to long for fall. That's when I got the idea. I want my bedroom to look like turning leaves."

That was easy enough, and it could be lovely. "Let me get some samples."

"No need." Sophie Ann pulled a picture from her purse.

"This is a picture I took when I visited New England during peak fall foliage two years ago."

Pam got a little lost in the grove of vibrant red, gold, yellow, and orange trees depicted in the picture. She could deal with a little fall herself.

The color palette began to take place in her mind. "You will want more muted tones than shown here, of course. And we can add some lovely mossy green and soft, earthy brown tones. It will be lovely."

"No," Sophie Ann said. "No brown, no green, no muted. I want bold colors just like these." She tapped her picture with her finger.

No. What was breathtaking on oak and maple trees in October would be a new category of ugly on a chair and wall.

"This would be *really* bright," Pam said.

"That's what I want. I want the room to come alive."

It would, all right. This room would look like a real live clown at a Halloween carnival. All that would be lacking would be a red light fixture for the nose. What Sophie Ann needed was to see the colors out of context.

"All right," Pam said because what else was there to say? "Just give me a minute to pull some fabric samples and paint chips so I can make sure we're on the same page."

Sophie Ann sighed. "All right. But hurry. I have a hair appointment at noon, and it's fifteen of now."

How had it gotten to be so late? She must have spent more time Internet-stalking Sammy than she'd thought.

"I'll just be a minute." The samples Pam pulled were meant only for accents, and they were bright enough to light the halls of hell. She hurried back and dumped the garish autumn rainbow on the coffee table in front of Sophie Ann. Surely when she saw it all together, she'd know how wrong it was. With any luck, she'd decide she wanted Annelle after all.

Or Lucy. Or the alley cat out back. Not that she was comparing Lucy to alley cat.

"Perfect!" Sophie Ann declared. "Just want I want." She picked up an intense maize paint chip. "This for the walls. Otherwise, use your judgment."

Lord, send a saint to deliver me. "How about a new overhead light fixture? I'm thinking round. In this color." Pam fingered a blaze-red sample.

"Yes. I like it. Hire the usual crew. Martha is there most days, but you can pick up a key from her if you need it." Martha was Sophie Ann's long-suffering housekeeper. Sophie Ann pointed her finger. "And, Pam? No greens and browns!"

And she bulldozed her way out the door like a woman with a hair roots emergency, which was probably the case.

Defeated, Pam bent to gather the samples. She'd have to make a file, and what, oh what, was Annelle going to say? She'd probably get fired.

"That woman does not want any greens and browns!" Sammy Anderson popped from behind the linen display case like a turbocharged jack-in-the-box and wagged his finger in an imitation of Sophie Ann.

Pam screamed and threw her arms up, sending Halloween clown colors sailing.

CHAPTER 4

Damn, damn, damn, damn.

Once again he'd done something stupid. That's what he got for trying to act like Gabe Beauford in an attempt to impress Pam. After some reflecting, Sammy had decided Gabe was about the most charming person he knew, at least with the kind of charm that made people smile and wish he would give them some of his time. Jumping out from behind something and making a joke was something Gabe would have done, only he would have made his audience like it—not scared her half to death. She dropped to her knees and reached under the couch.

"I am so sorry!" Sammy rushed to help Pam pick up her little pieces of cloth and color squares. "I didn't mean to scare you."

"Where did you come from?" She sounded breathless, which only added to her appeal. And she was so appealing. She hadn't lost a bit of cute, especially with her hair flying and her hands darting around trying to bring order to the chaos he'd caused.

She was like music in his head.

"When I came in, that woman was sitting on the couch and you were busy in the back." (The cuddle couch. Apparently they did let people sit on it, but probably not him.) "I just figured I'd go over there and look at things until you were done." There had been plenty to look at, too—all kinds of little dishes, lamps, napkins, and pillows. It all made about as much sense to Sammy as an airplane parts store, and who could have guessed that sheets cost so much?

Then they both reached for a square of orange and their fingers brushed. Before Sammy could stop himself, he grabbed her hand. The warm waves he'd remembered from before hadn't just been in his imagination, and today they carried him off to sea. She looked at their hands and then raised her eyes to his.

That's when his natural talent for caretaking kicked in. She was rattled and he could fix that. She tried to pull her hand away, but he squeezed it and put his other hand under her elbow.

"Here." He raised her to her feet and guided her to the couch. "You just sit right here and catch your breath. I'll pick up this mess."

"It's okay. I'll get it." She started to rise again.

"No. I've got it." He put his hand on her knee. He shouldn't have, but the waves felt good; they lifted his heart, and his heart had never been lifted before. How was that possible? "I'll clean this up, and then I need to do something to make up for being me."

She wrinkled her brow and went from cute to mega cute. And then she decided to smile. Sammy had observed that there were two kinds of smiles—a willful one and one that can't be helped. He would take either.

"Do you often feel that you have to make up for being you?"

"You have no idea." He felt a can't-help-it smile coming on.

"I might," she said.

"I'm sure that's not true." And it couldn't be.

His hand remained on her knee. Her pants were thin enough that he could feel the warmth of her skin through them. He needed to move his hand because he'd promised her he would pick up her scattered things.

He reluctantly moved away from her and began cleaning up the mess.

"I suppose you came by to talk about the concert," Pam said.

"We *do* need to talk about that." But in truth, the reason he'd come here first, even before going to Missy's to unload his stuff, was because he'd wanted to. "I need to see this farm and stake off where the stage needs to go." He settled on the sofa beside her and began to sort the color cards from the fabric squares. "Maybe we could go to lunch? And then, if you have time, go take a look at the venue?"

She shook her head and disappointment washed over him. "I can't. Annelle and Lucy are in Atlanta today, and they depend on me. The college student who works here part time will be here in a bit, but I shouldn't leave her alone."

"I understand." And he did. She didn't want to go. He set about arranging the fabric and cards into excruciatingly orderly stacks.

"You don't have to stack those up so neatly. I have to go through them again later anyway."

He continued to line up edges. His stomach growled loudly.

"You must be hungry."

He nodded. "I usually stop in Decatur and eat hamburgers at this place that's been there for nearly a hundred years."

Her head popped up. "Penn's?"

"Yes! You've had it?" This was too good to be true.

"More times than I should have." She pulled at the tail of her pretty pink, silky shirt. "I'm just thankful they aren't available here. I have an aunt who lives in Decatur. She says when she was a little girl, they only had burgers, milk, and soft drinks in bottles. They didn't even have cheeseburgers. It was later when they added french fries, hot dogs, and the other stuff."

"Might as well not have, for my money. I don't bother with any of that. Do you get yours all the way?"

"Yes. And I add ketchup."

So she was an onion eater. He'd heard if you both ate onions, you couldn't taste it on each other.

"Not me. I eat them like the original Mr. Penn intended."

"Why didn't you stop today?" she asked.

He'd thought about it, thought about getting them without the onions, but decided it wouldn't be the same. Looks like he should have stopped after all. She didn't want to eat lunch with him.

But what the hell? Why not tell her the real reason he didn't stop? He didn't have anything to lose. "Maybe I wanted to get here. Maybe I was excited about seeing you."

She blushed bright red and looked at the floor. *Well, knock me over with a feather.* She thought he was teasing her, maybe even making fun of her! As unthinkable as that was, he guessed he could see why. He'd sounded like he was teasing, but that was for self-protection—and that didn't make what he'd said any less true.

He didn't understand a lot about this situation and the way he was feeling. And, for certain, nothing had changed about Pam being out of his league—but it didn't seem like she knew it.

Maybe he could have her. Was that remotely possible? Her coloring was returning to normal, but she still didn't seem to want to look at him. The warm waves crashed around his heart.

He was going to have to be very careful with her. Plenty of women—mostly music people—had drifted through his bed, but none he'd needed to be careful with.

"It's probably better not to go straight out to that farm now, anyway," he said. "You're wearing your pretty clothes and nice shoes. Could you go later? After you get off work and after it cools down some?" Then he had a bad thought, one that made the warm waves freeze. Why had he not considered that she might be in a relationship? "Unless, that is … you probably have someone you spend evenings with." But he still had a job to do. "In that case, you might draw me a map." He really did have to stake out the stage and look around for snakes. It wouldn't do to let a concertgoer get bitten by a diamondback rattler. That almost never ended well.

Her eyes widened before understanding spread over her face.

"No. I mean, I'm free. I'm always free. I can do that."

Relief. Sweet relief. He might better take a hoe to defend her against snakes.

"Would you like to get dinner, too? You know, so I can make up for being me?" He gestured to the neat stacks on the table.

She laughed. "Sure. I can be ready by six."

"It's a date," he said. And he hoped that was true. "I'll pick you up."

CHAPTER 5

Pam surveyed her closet for something to wear. She didn't want to think of this as a date, regardless of what Sammy had said. Just because he'd been flirty didn't mean he'd meant *date* in the romantic sense, or even the social sense. Date could also mean an arranged time to meet to do work. The common love of Penn's hamburgers was not a basis for attraction, and she'd do well to remember that.

As far back as eleventh grade, she and Colton Reeves had both liked brownies, but when she'd gained some weight, he'd broken up with her a week before the prom—and told her why. It hadn't helped when her mother had pointed out that she'd brought it on herself and her father offered to pay for fat camp. Neither Tripp Bentley in college nor Shawn Faulkner two years ago had been as candid as Colton, but they'd both turned up with prettier, thinner girls after giving the it's-not-you-I'm-just-not-ready speeches. There had been a few other failed attempts at relationships, but those three were the highlights—the ones she'd slept with and the ones she'd thought might turn into something long lasting.

AND NOT A SINGLE ONE OF THEM WAS AS SHOWSTOPPING, HEAD-TURNING GORGEOUS AS SAMMY, NOR HAD THEY BEEN PART OF A BIG, GLAMOROUS, STAR-FILLED LIFE. IT MIGHT NOT EXACTLY BE SAMMY'S LIFE, BUT IT WAS CLOSE ENOUGH. AND SHE HAD NOT BEEN ANYWHERE NEARLY AS ATTRACTED TO ANY OF THEM AS SHE WAS TO SAMMY.

SHE HADN'T HAD A DATE SINCE SHAWN, AND SHE PROBABLY WASN'T HAVING ONE TONIGHT.

What to wear, what to wear? She needed to look nice, but not too nice. After all, they were going to tromp around on Luke and Lanie Avery's farm. Surely he wasn't expecting to go to dinner at a place where they needed to be dressed better than one would dress for farm tromping. There were only two places in town that would require that—the Merritt Inn and the country club. But who knew what he expected? Well, she'd dress for farm tromping and cross that bridge if she came to it.

It was too hot for jeans, and a skirt was out of the question, as were nice linen pants. She had a couple of pairs of cropped pants that would have been appropriate, but they were dirty, and there wasn't time to do laundry.

That left knee-length fat shorts and golf shirts—meaning that both garments were two sizes too big for her, thus providing plenty of coverage for her thighs and bottom. She had several such outfits, but she felt most confident and comfortable in the khaki shorts and navy shirt. Plain gold earrings, Keds and no-show socks, and a little blush and lip gloss. There. Not too bad. Good enough for a non-date.

Now, if she could just get out of the house before her

mother got back from playing tennis. Her dad was in Birmingham today and wouldn't be back until late, so she would be spared the possibility of Sammy seeing her with two perfect people. Why hadn't she suggested that they meet?

That's when it hit her. When he said he'd pick her up, he hadn't asked where she lived, and it had never occurred to her to tell him. This was Merritt. Everyone knew where everyone else lived. And as far as she knew, he didn't have her phone number.

So maybe they weren't going at all. Or maybe he'd meant he'd pick her up at the shop. Should she go back over there?

That's when the doorbell rang.

At least she'd gotten the dress code right. He wore cargo shorts, Converse tennis shoes, and a faded Jackson Beauford T-shirt that hugged his muscles in way that left nothing to the imagination. And she could imagine a lot.

But she shouldn't let herself imagine that his smile got brighter and sweeter when she opened the door. She shouldn't imagine putting her tongue in his dimple.

Stop it! Stop thinking things like that. Thinking leads to doing, and then you'd have to kill yourself.

But she could almost taste the salt on his face and feel the warmth.

Her expression must have shown what she thought. Why else would be he cocking his head to the side and narrowing his eyes? Looking at her like every woman longs to be looked at? Ogling even. That was it! It was a pity ogle. She'd heard of pity sex, but this was a whole new level of pathetic.

"Hey, Pam." His voice was like molasses, which was one of her favorite things. It alone probably accounted for at least ten of her excess thirty pounds.

"Do you like molasses?" she blurted out and died inside. That settled it. She couldn't be trusted to have a tongue—not for talking and not for licking dimples. She was going to go straight inside and cut it out.

"Well, yeah!" He feigned shock. "What fool doesn't? I like it on biscuits and ice cream. But you know what I don't like? I don't like honey. Not at all. I'd rather have Karo syrup than honey. You know. If there's no molasses."

"I like honey, too." This conversation was all her fault, and she did not know how to stop it. What's more, he was still on the porch and she was on the other side of the threshold.

"You can. I will not fault you for it. But you can have all the honey in the world that has been allotted to me. It's all yours." He smiled broader and leaned on the doorjamb. "Should we go? Or would you like to move on to jams, jellies, and preserves? Not everyone knows the difference in those things, but I do. I have spent a lot of time with Gwen, who does not hold with buying food readymade in a store, but believes very much in schooling me on a variety of topics."

And just like that, Pam was at ease. He was so sweet, so funny. And he wasn't making fun of her at all. She might never be allowed to put her tongue in his dimple, but it was just so nice to be around him. It was enough. She'd gotten used to *enough* a long time ago.

"I met Gwen when I went to Beauford Bend with Lucy to install window treatments."

"You mean hang curtains?"

"More or less. Would you like to come in or should we go?"

"I'll come in next time. Jackson told me about a diner downtown. He says it's the best."

"Lou Anne's." Pam picked up her purse from the foyer table and locked the door behind her. "Everyone goes there."

"I checked. It's open late. If you're not too hungry, I thought we might go look at the property before we eat. Then we can relax and won't have to hurry over dinner."

"Sounds good." But didn't everything?

No. Not everything—not the sound of her mother's Lexus turning into the driveway just as she and Sammy were about to step off the porch. Pam caught her breath. If they hurried, maybe they could escape. Her mother didn't always get out of the car right away. She often checked her phone, applied lipstick, sometimes returned a call.

But no such luck today. She shot out of the car like a bull out of the chute at a rodeo—only there was nothing bull-like about her, especially in her tennis dress. She was tan, long-legged, and fit. She looked at least ten years younger than her actual age, something that didn't often go with tan.

There was nothing to do but stop. She was practically upon them.

"Hello, Mother."

"On your way somewhere?" Leslie Carson might have been speaking to Pam, but her eyes were on Sammy. Pam knew exactly what was going through her mind. She was torn between appreciating his beauty and being appalled at how he was dressed. Most of all, she was astounded that Sammy was here with Pam—the last born and biggest disappointment of her three children.

"Yes. We're on our way to the Avery farm to look at the concert site."

"Ah." Leslie glanced at Pam, nodded with understanding and, again, rested her eyes on Sammy. She might as well have said, *"So it's business. That explains it. There is no way that chubby, uneducated, underachieving Pam could have landed a date with someone who looks like him, even if he is wearing red tennis shoes and a T-shirt that talks."*

"Mother, this is Sammy Anderson. Sammy, my mother. Leslie Carson. Mother, Sammy is here representing Jackson Beauford."

"So nice to meet you." Leslie advanced on him with her hand extended.

"And you." Sammy shook her hand. "I understand you were a concert pianist. My mother plays piano."

What? How did he know that?

"Oh?" Leslie said. "Professionally?"

He laughed, all charming. "No, unless you count giving lessons to kids at the house. But she plays at church."

Leslie nodded. "Admirable. I couldn't do that."

"Me either," Sammy said. "But for a different reason. No talent. She tried hard to teach me, but she didn't try long. She always could see the writing on the wall."

Leslie nodded and turned to Pam. "Russ and I are going to dinner at the club. Should I bring you something for later? Maybe a salad or some broiled fish."

Great. Point out in front of Sammy that she needed to lose weight, just in case he hadn't noticed. "No thank you, Mother. Sammy and I are going to get something at Lou Anne's when we're finished at the farm."

"Oh. Lou Anne's. Well. But speaking of the concert, Pam, we need three more tickets."

Pam was already shaking her head. "I don't have three tickets to give you. Besides, why do you need more? You and Daddy bought tickets when they went on sale."

"That's the best news! Kurt and Angie are coming down. And Angie's brother Miller is coming with them. Won't it be nice to see him?"

That again. Her parents had finally faced that Pam wasn't going to finish college or achieve anything on her own, so they had decided she must achieve by marriage—namely to her sister-in-law's brother who had invented some scientific process that had apparently been a very big deal to people who cared, of which she was not one.

"I don't think I will see him, Mother. I am going to be too

busy that weekend to see anyone." Except Sammy, who would be just as busy. They'd be busy together. She hoped.

"Surely after the whole thing gets underway, you can join us for the concert."

Pam shook her head. "Even if I could, there aren't any tickets for them. I have some for corporate sponsors and volunteers, but I'm cutting it close as it is."

"Surely you can do something. You're running the whole thing! You brother has already booked a flight."

She wanted to scream. "Mother …"

"I can help," Sammy said. "Give me second." And he sprinted down the sidewalk to his truck.

"He has tickets?"

"Apparently." Pam leaned in and hissed in her mother's ear. "Listen to me, Mother, and listen well. Sammy will be right back, and I won't discuss this in front of him. I am not interested in Angie's brother. I am not going to cooperate. I mean it."

"Pam—"

"Here you go, Mrs. Carson." Sammy appeared again. "These are family and friends passes." He held out five bright yellow, laminated passes on lanyards. "There will be comfortable seating near the stage with a bar and special food. One of my jobs is to keep up with how much seating is needed and do the set up." He looked at Pam. "Don't worry about this. We have our own tables and chairs and provide the food. It's standard."

"So this is where Jackson's wife sits? And brothers?" Why did she not know about this? And what else didn't she know?

Sammy nodded. "And the wives and Gwen. Missy and her family. I give out the passes."

"And they are going to be all right with this?"

Sammy nodded. "They trust me."

"Well, I cannot thank you enough," Leslie said.

"But they only need three," Pam said, though she knew there was no way her mother was going to give up this special perk.

Sammy nodded. "I thought maybe it would help you out if your mom gave you her tickets, since you're worried you won't have enough."

"Well, yes." Leslie was as pleased as she ever was.

"Mrs. Carson," Sammy said, "I will have to ask you not to tell anyone about these. When people find out I control the passes, they can get very annoying."

"Don't worry. I won't."

And Pam knew that was true. Leslie wouldn't want anyone else to be shown the same favor.

As they made their way down the walk, Pam said, "That was nice of you."

"I *am* nice. Everyone says so." He winked at her.

Then he opened the passenger door of his truck. She reached for the grab handle, but her hand never made it there.

"I've got you." He put his arms around her waist and lifted her before she could protest. It seemed that he might have held on a little longer than necessary, but still not long enough to suit her.

CHAPTER 6

"The farm has been in the Avery family for a long time. Luke Avery's father is a state senator and Luke's parents spend most of the year in Montgomery." Pam thought she sounded a little like a tour guide on a double-decker bus, but Sammy seemed interested. "Luke lived in Mobile, but moved to Merritt with his little girl when his first wife died. After he married Lanie, they moved to the farm."

"Is Lanie the one with the candy shop?"

"Yes. Heavenly Confections. All the candy is made in house."

"Does she have fudge?" Sammy asked. "I love fudge."

"All kinds. Milk chocolate, dark chocolate, white chocolate, peanut butter. Some with nuts and dried fruit."

"I wouldn't have thought about fruit in fudge, but I'm willing to try it."

"I try to stay out of there." Pam pulled at her shirttail.

"Nonsense. I'll take you there. We'll try it all. I suppose it would be too much to hope for that she makes it right in the front window like they do in Gatlinburg. Have you ever seen that?"

"Yes, I have. And yes, that would be too much to hope for. Lanie makes her candy in the kitchen." She couldn't keep the smile out of her voice. She could imagine Sammy on a crowded Gatlinburg sidewalk mesmerized by the candy makers. "Does Gwen make fudge?"

He sighed. "Not nearly often enough. My mother can't make fudge. She doesn't even try anymore. How about you? Can you make fudge?"

With him giving her that part sexy, part sweet sidelong look, it was tempting to lie, but no good would come from that.

"Yes." She returned his smile. "Though not as good as Lanie's."

"Do you wear an apron when you make it?" he asked.

"Uh, no. I don't have an apron."

"I'll buy you one if you'll make me some fudge."

That was odd. "Or we could just buy fudge. The turn is coming up. Next right."

He swung the truck into the mile-long, tree-lined drive. "This looks a lot like the drive to Beauford Bend."

"The tree canopy makes it feel like we're in a cool, magical forest."

Sammy nodded. "I'll bet it's really pretty in the fall. It is at Beauford Bend."

"Yes," Pam said. "Though I may never look at fall the same way again."

"Why? Did something bad happen to you in the fall?"

"Not yet. It might be coming. The client I was with when you came into the shop earlier—"

"The one who does not want any greens and browns?"

"Yes." She and Sammy laughed quietly together, and with that companionable laughter came a feeling of bonding. She'd never felt that way before, and she wondered if he felt it, too.

He lightly laid a hand on hers. "So how has she ruined fall for you?"

"She wants her bedroom done in true shades of autumn leaves."

"That's bad?"

"Oh, yes. It'll be hideous. A Halloween carnival clown is what came to mind. She won't allow me to do anything to tone it down. I tried to tell her."

"I don't know anything about that. But I know this: you've done all you can. When your job is doing other people's bidding, all you can do is try to tell them. If you still disagree, you just have to do what they say. I love Jackson Beauford like a brother, and he has been good to me, but a more stubborn man has never been born. More than once, he's had to eat his words."

"I do not love Sophie Ann McGowan, and she has not been good to me. She is not one to eat words. But you're right about one thing. I have no choice but to carry on and make a clown room."

Just then the house came into view. Though more homey and restful than grand, in size, the white wood structure was more mansion than farmhouse.

"Look. There's someone on the porch." Sammy stopped the truck.

"That's Lanie." She was watering the flowers in her window boxes.

"I should say hello," he said. "I'll be quick." Though she didn't touch the controls, Pam's window went down. "So you can talk without getting out."

And he swung out of the truck and began to walk toward Lanie, who had seen them and was coming down the porch steps. They stopped right outside Pam's window.

"Sammy Anderson." He shook Lanie's hand. "Mrs. Avery,

Jackson wanted me to express his appreciation to you and Judge Avery."

"Our pleasure. And please, we're Luke and Lanie." She smiled Pam's way and raised an eyebrow. "How are you, Pam? Emma will be so sorry she missed you, but after art camp, she and John Luke went home with Missy to swim."

"I'm sorry to have missed her, too. We need an ice cream date."

"*I* need an ice cream date," Sammy said.

"I thought you needed a fudge date," Pam said. "Lanie, Sammy was telling me how much he likes fudge. I told him yours is the best."

"Come by and sample. It's on the house."

"The only thing better than fudge is free fudge," Sammy said. "I hope it's all right that we came out. I want to look over the concert site."

"Absolutely," Lanie said. "Come any time. Pam knows the location."

"I'll let you know exactly when we expect the stage company, but I will be around to supervise every minute they're here. I'll make sure they don't go near your house or park on your lawn. If there's anything else that's off limits, let me know."

Lanie shook her head. "I can't think of anything. Feel free to use the barn for whatever you need. Missy mentioned putting the caterers in there. It has electricity and running water. We don't keep animals. The senior classes use it to build homecoming floats every fall, and we use it when we have fish fries and such. It's pretty clean—at least for a barn."

"I appreciate that." To Pam's surprise, Sammy removed what looked to be an antique sterling silver card case from his pocket and handed Lanie a card. "Here's my contact information. I'm staying at Missy Bragg's in her pool house. Please don't hesitate to contact me if you have any concerns or questions. But I promise you, Lanie, I'll take care of your property as if it were Beauford Bend."

"I have no concerns at all," Lanie said. "That's a beautiful card case."

"Thank you. It was a gift."

A gift from a girl. No doubt about it. Pam wished it had been a gift from her.

"If I can't do anything for you, make yourselves at home," Lanie said. "Call if you have any questions."

"She was nice." Sammy restarted the truck. "Is she your close friend?"

"I wouldn't say that, though I like her and I've known her for a long time. Go straight down this road until I tell you to turn. The year I got sent home from Jacksonville State, I worked part time for Annelle and babysat for Emma. That was when Lanie and Luke were dating. They were always good to me."

"Sent home from Jacksonville State? That sounds like it wasn't your choice."

Damn. She hadn't meant to say that. Oh, well.

"Not my choice, but it was a relief. I was on academic probation."

Sammy looked at her, surprised. "I wouldn't have thought that was possible. You're so smart."

Might as well tell him. "Not really. At least I'm not a good student. I never was. I can't explain it, but I don't care. I like what I'm doing and I'm good at it. Annelle and Lucy appreciate me. So why does it matter?"

She sounded like she was arguing with herself.

Sammy shrugged. "It doesn't matter to me. And I understand. I wasn't a good student either. And I wasn't always good at what I do. But I am now."

"My parents don't share your view. I'm twenty-four years old, and they only recently accepted that I'm not going back to college."

Sammy smiled. "I never went at all."

"Turn left up ahead. See the barn? We can use any of this area to the tree line."

"Not bad. Great, in fact. It's clear and freshly mown. I was afraid I'd have to get a bush hog out here before I could even measure. I'll come back in the morning and stake out the stage, but I want to walk around." He pulled onto the gravel beside the barn.

"There's plenty of room for parking." Pam unbuckled her seatbelt.

"Too bad only this small part has gravel. Unless there's a dangerous storm, we wouldn't call the show on account of rain, but parking could be a problem. Can't have a bunch of cars sunk in the mud up to their axles. We'll have to have a rain plan."

Pam's stomach sank. "I never thought about that! How stupid! Oh, God. I should have never taken this on."

"Hey." Sammy laid his hand on her wrist. "This ain't my first rodeo. I've got you. We'll make a rain plan. It's not as hard as you think. It will probably involve finding an alternate parking facility—maybe the high school—and renting some shuttle buses."

"Missy doesn't like to spend money."

"It might come down to either renting shuttle buses or refunding a whole lot of people a whole lot of money. Guess which one we're going to pick. And Missy's not in charge anymore. We are."

He sounded so calm, so sure. She liked being part of his *we*.

"All right." She reached for her door handle.

"Keep your seat, please."

What? Did he not intend to let her walk around the site with him?

But then he opened her door. "Swing your legs around, but don't get out." He knelt down and started removing her right shoe.

"What are you doing?"

He reached into a canvas bag beside him on the ground. "Putting some real socks on you." He waved one of her no-show socks in the air. "These are cute, but they don't protect against chiggers."

"Chiggers?"

"Oh, come on. You might be a city girl, but you're from the South. You know what chiggers are." He put an ugly athletic sock on her and pulled it up to her knee.

"Of course I know what chiggers are. I just didn't think." She shuddered at the thought of the miniscule pests that burrowed into the skin, causing welts and unbearable itching.

"Sure you did, just not about this." He put her shoe back on and tied it. "You were thinking about the impossible Sophie May."

"Sophie Ann. And why didn't you just send me back for long pants?"

He removed her other shoe and ran his hand up her calf. "What? Am I stupid? And miss the sight of this? I don't think so."

Her whole being was swimming with the stars—and all for a hand on her calf. She tried, tried hard, to key into that sometimes-unwelcome sixth sense, but it was useless. She couldn't read Sammy, had no idea if he was feeding her a line.

She was speechless, but cast around for something—anything—to say. "You aren't wearing tall socks or long pants."

"I was built to fight all manner of vermin," he said. "I don't care if I get chiggers. My mother used to strip me down and use Scotch tape to get them off me, which is why I have Scotch tape in my bag."

She might be willing to do that for him.

"Now." He put on the second athletic sock and replaced her shoe. "Let's get you sprayed now."

"Sprayed?"

He pulled a can of insect repellent from his bag. "I'm going to spray your shoes first. There. A little on each knee. That's good. Hold out your arms."

"Are you always so prepared?"

"Always. Sit tight while I get my hoe."

"Hoe?" Surely he didn't have a prostitute in the back of that truck. But these *were* music people. She laughed at the ridiculous thought. At least she hoped it was ridiculous.

He walked to the back of his truck and, to her relief, came back with a garden hoe.

"What are you going to do with that?"

He smiled wide and happy. "Kill snakes if I have to. Or coyotes." He leaned the hoe against the truck and held out his arms. "Come here and let me help you. This is a great big truck, and you're just a little thing."

Little thing? "Oh, no, I can—"

But before he could finish, she was in his arms and sliding down the length of his warm, firm body until her feet touched the ground.

But he still didn't release her. And this time it was *not* her imagination. She tried to pull away, but he angled his head and looked at her. His hair fell in his eyes.

"Sammy, what—"

He didn't say anything for a beat. He just looked at her.

Then he spoke, low and sweet. "Not right here and not right now, but before this night is over, I'm going to kiss you. You know that, don't you?"

"No. I didn't—" She would have thought she would have

been lightheaded at such a moment, but she was far from it—probably because she wanted to savor every second while it lasted. But she was confused, so confused.

"I am. I will. I wanted to before. When we first met. But I had eaten all those onions, you see. I'd had three Penn's hamburgers."

"Oh! I thought … I mean I thought I'd misunderstood." She hadn't been wrong! He had been about to kiss her that day in the storeroom.

"I don't think you misunderstand much. But I just wanted to give you fair warning that I want to finish what I started. I have wanted to kiss you for three months. And I intend to do it. Soon. Tonight."

She shook her head, maybe in wonder, maybe in denial. "Sammy, please don't play with me. Don't make me like you more than I should."

But, really, don't listen to me. Lie to me. Kiss me. Leave me in the dirt if you have to when this concert is over, but let me have this.

He shook his head. "No, Pam. If there's a heart at stake here, it's mine. You might be wondering why I don't just kiss you instead of talking about it. I want to anticipate it, without worrying that you'll cut and run. You won't, will you." There wasn't a question mark in his voice.

But she answered anyway. "No. I wouldn't run. I'm not athletic."

He made a sound, part laugh, part *hmm.* "Good. I don't want you running from me. I know you probably think this is fast, but I can't help it. I didn't think I had a chance with you, and maybe I don't, but I have to try."

He didn't think he had a chance with *her.*

"I've always moved too slow, always second-guessed myself. But I spent three months thinking about you. When I found out I was coming back, I decided it was a sign."

Pam wasn't sure if it was a dream or a nightmare. It was one thing to fantasize about this, but another for it to seem to be happening.

"You don't know anything about me," she said.

"Of course I do. I Googled you."

"You Googled me! That's how you knew where I live." And that her mother had been a concert pianist.

"Of course." He laughed. "Don't worry, it's not like I hired a private investigator. Everything I found out was on the Internet."

"Still..." Since she'd done her share of Googling, she didn't have much room for indignation.

"I can't explain it. I couldn't get you off my mind, and it was something to do."

She understood that well enough—if he was telling the truth. But how could he be? She searched his eyes. They looked honest.

"You have eyes like Bambi," she said.

"Do what?"

"Bambi. That's what I told Audrey the day you walked in the shop."

A cocky little smile spread across his face. "You talked about me?"

"Maybe." Why didn't she shut up?

"Deer have brown eyes. Mine are blue."

"I'm well aware. It's the lashes."

"Ah. The lashes." He hadn't let her go all this time, and now he pulled her tighter in and the embrace took on a different tone—if an embrace could have a tone. She became aware of his thighs against hers. "I'm feeling a little insecure here. I love having my arms around you, but do you think you could return the favor?"

It was only then that she realized, though she was tight against him, she was hanging in his arms like a rag doll.

Gingerly, she raised her arms and encircled his waist. This was different from anything she'd ever experienced before, holding and being held by this man who was so sure and so capable. Maybe that was the difference. She'd only been with boys before, but Sammy was a man.

"Relax," he whispered against her ear. "Don't think. Just feel it. This is the first time we've been in each other's arms. We won't get another first."

What woman wouldn't melt at those words? She let the tension and the doubts go. Doubting and second-guessing was a waste of energy anyway, because she was already gone. She flattened her hands against his back and slid them up his shoulders and down again.

He let out a low moan and stroked her hair, tilting her head back the tiniest bit. "I think … No. *I know.* I am going to kiss you now—right damn now."

And he brought his mouth down on hers, sweet with just the right amount of demanding. Crickets sang the twilight song, and somewhere in the distance a lawnmower hummed. The worst of day's heat had faded, but the metal of Sammy's truck was still warm on Pam's back. Without taking his mouth from hers, he propped a foot on the running board and brought her pelvis closer in to his. Though he was spectacularly rigid and throbbing so hard that she felt him through their clothes, he did not grind against her. Perfectly intent on the kiss, he explored her mouth thoroughly with his tongue, and then gently coaxed hers into his mouth.

Slow, tender, thorough. This was like every first kiss that anyone had ever dreamed of. Even if she'd tried, she would not have been able to remember any past kisses.

This was a real kiss—*the* kiss. And she never wanted it to end.

But it did, of course. People couldn't kiss forever. But

when they parted, he leaned his forehead against hers, and that was so nice.

"Just in case you didn't know, I want you." His voice was breathless and heavy. "Really bad."

"I suspected." Did he think she didn't know a raging hard-on when she felt one? True, she didn't think she'd ever felt one quite that size, but still. "Sorry about that." But he did nothing to distance to the evidence of his desire from where it was pressed against her. In fact, he might have rolled his hips just a bit, sending a shock wave through her. And she might have answered in kind.

"Thor's thunder, girl."

"Well … You started it."

"I really wanted it to be romantic and all about the kiss, but you do something to me, something really fine and sweet."

"It *was* romantic and all about the kiss." She felt him jerk against her. "Well, mostly." She slid her hand up the back of his neck and let her fingertips caress his hairline.

He shuddered. "If I was listening to parts south, I'd take you in that barn and have my way with you right now."

Actually, that didn't sound like a bad idea. It was probably dark enough that she could take her clothes off. There is no way she could let him see her pudgy self in full light.

His hair was thick and silky, and his neck hot and a little damp. She played there for a bit, until he closed his eyes and let his head roll back. Then he shook his head and looked at her again.

"Right. The barn. You and me. But I'm not going to do that." He reached up and drew her hand away from his neck and squeezed it. "I'm *not* going have sex with you the same day I first kiss you." It sounded like he was talking more to himself than her.

Wonder how many hours until midnight. But she couldn't say that.

"I'm going to be careful with you," Sammy said. "You're special, so special that I don't want to make any mistakes. You deserve the best. I can't be the best, but I can give you the best I've got."

It was the most romantic moment of her life. It always would be. Nothing could top those words, even if he didn't mean them, even if he'd said them to a thousand other women.

"So here's what's going to happen," he continued. "I'm going to take you to eat. Then I'm going to take you home. I don't want to, but I am." He drew away from her and took her other hand. "By then, it will be good and dark. Before I let you out of my truck, I plan to kiss you some more. And I hope you'll do that thing with your hand on the back of my neck again. That's new. I didn't know about that." He looked her up and down with a pained expression. "I'm probably going to do everything to you that I can without taking our clothes off."

And I'm probably going to let you.

How on earth was she supposed to be able to eat after a promise like that?

"And, Pam?" His cornflower blue eyes widened. "I'm going to follow your lead. I won't press you to have sex. I don't want to mess this up before it even starts. You have to tell me when you're ready."

And how would she ever be able to do that? She had never taken the lead in much, let alone sex. Truth be told, if he'd pressed her, she would have happily gone to that barn with him tonight, without any thought to whether she was ready. But it seemed now that was a question she was going to have to consider.

CHAPTER 7

Sammy was in deep, so deep. Not literally, of course, though he wanted to be; wanted it more than he ever had—and he had the aching balls to prove it. And that wasn't going to get any better.

But he'd had a taste of her now, and he could not make mistakes he couldn't come back from. He'd watched every single one of the Beaufords come within a hair of messing up, and he was not going to be that guy.

Pam sat across from him in a booth at Lou Anne's Diner.

"You didn't explore the property." She picked at her salad.

No. He'd been too busy exploring her mouth and trying to talk himself out of exploring other parts of her.

"I sort of forgot."

Pam smiled, clearly pleased that she'd made him forget what he had gone there for. He wanted to reach across the table and take her hand, but he was afraid if he did, he'd be right back in the shape he'd been in when they'd left the Avery farm. No. He didn't dare touch her.

"I'll do it tomorrow. I need to look around for anthills

and wasp nests and snakes, but the property is in good shape. We'll have to spray for mosquitoes."

Her eyes widened, and she covered her mouth with her hand—the hand he wanted to hold. He's already learned that gesture meant she was surprised. She was probably appalled that she hadn't thought of that. He'd sidetrack her from the feeling with a compliment. He'd seen Gabe do it a thousand times.

"I like your hands." Her nails were short, neat, and shiny. "I don't like long nails with all that purple and green nail polish."

"No?" She studied her nails. "I don't wear colored polish at all. I think it's distracting when I'm showing a customer fabric swatches and paint chips."

"You're good at your job."

"And you're good at yours. How did you come to work for Jackson Beauford?"

"I never did; not officially. When I was in high school, I started working for Miss Amelia, Jackson's great aunt. She ran Around the Bend, the party business. I washed dishes, helped set up tents and chairs. That kind of thing. Eventually, they let me serve at parties. After I graduated, I stayed on. I didn't know how to do anything else, and eventually they hired me full time. After Miss Amelia died, Emory gave me more duties. That was way before she and Jackson got together."

"So like me, you fell into it and just kept doing it?" Pam said.

"I've never thought about it like that, but I suppose so. I still can't believe they kept me, because in the beginning, I was terrible. I'd forget things. Break things. Say the wrong thing. It's a wonder I didn't get fired. In fact, I almost did once. There was this wedding going on. A couple of the groomsmen told me Emory said it would be okay to show them Jackson's private suite. I would never fall for such a thing now, but I'd been taught to make the guests happy, so I let them in. They went wild and I couldn't get them out. Drank his beer. Drank a fancy bottle of bourbon that Willie Nelson gave Jackson when Jackson was inducted into the Grand Ole Opry. But worst of all, they went in his music room where he keeps his guitar collection. They took the ones that had belonged to Chet Atkins and Jimi Hendrix out of their display cases and started strumming them." Thinking about it now made his stomach churn.

Pam put her hand over her mouth. "Oh, dear. Really?"

He nodded. "Worth a fortune and worth more than that to Jackson. Lucky for me, they didn't hurt the guitars, or Jackson would have probably killed me. Well, it just so happened that was the night Jackson returned to Beauford Bend after that fire at his concert in California where all those people died."

Pam nodded. "I remember that."

"He was in no mood for foolishness to begin with, and he was fit to be tied. He tried to make Emory fire me, but she wouldn't, though she did take my master key. For a while, they fought every morning before breakfast. But after that, Jackson and I got friendly. I could grill a steak the way he liked it. I could iron his pants, and I'd wash his truck and gas it up before he realized it needed to be done. Eventually, I learned to anticipate what he wanted."

"So that's when you stopped working for Around the Bend?"

"Not exactly. We all do what has to be done. And I live on the property, so I'm always handy."

She frowned. "So they just shuffled you around without even asking you?"

That sounded bad. He took a bite of his meatloaf and reflected on that while he chewed.

"It wasn't like that. It just kind of … evolved."

"You're so good at what you do. I saw that today. You think of everything. That's a talent. You could do anything you wanted, even start your own business."

"My own business?" That was crazy talk. "Doing what?"

"Anything that interests you. What you do is anticipate and manage."

"And I'm good at it. But I *am* doing what interests me, where I want to do it."

"And it doesn't bother you that they send you to pick up rugs?"

"Why would it bother me? They have needs. I fulfill those needs. I am paid the same whether I'm picking up rugs, taking Gwen on a hell ride hunting organic goat cheese, or going ahead of Jackson and Emory to a fancy New York hotel to make sure everything is like he wants it. Besides, on that particular rug-fetching errand I got to lay my eyes on the cutest girl I've ever seen. And I get the feeling I might have a chance with her."

She blushed deep red and looked at her plate.

He was tired of talking about himself. "How about you? Wouldn't you like to have your own shop?"

She shook her head. "Under different circumstances I might, but I can't. I can't call myself an interior designer. That takes a degree, experience, and passing a state-regulated exam."

Sammy's fork, and the piece of fried green tomato he'd just stabbed with it, clattered to his plate. "To pick out cloth? That's the dumbest thing I've ever heard in my life." Her face clouded, and he regretted it immediately. "Not that picking cloth is easy. No, sir. I couldn't do it."

"There are reasons for the requirements. It's important to understand safety codes for commercial work. For example, you couldn't use the same products in a hospital that would be fine in a residence."

"Okay. I believe you."

"Besides, Merritt couldn't support more than one interior design shop, even if I could call myself a designer."

Before Sammy could point out that Merritt wasn't the only place on the planet, a woman approached the table.

"Hello, Pam," she said, but her eyes were on him. Sammy knew her type. Tall, blond, hollow-cheeked, with sharp hipbones. She would think her cleavage and pouty lips would buy her something.

Pam said, "Hello, Alexandria." She looked like an Alexandria. That was a name that would wear a man's tongue out. Probably wouldn't let people call her Alex or Sandy.

"What have we here?" She looked Sammy up and down.

He stood, probably not as fast as Miss Amelia would have wanted him to, but she'd give him credit for eventually remembering his manners.

"Sammy Anderson."

"Yes," Pam said. "Alexandria, this is Sammy Anderson. Sammy, Alexandria Keeton. We went to high school together. Alexandria, Sammy works for Jackson Beauford. He's here to consult about the benefit concert."

"Ohhhh," she said like people did when they found out who he was associated with. "In that case …" She picked up a napkin from the table and scribbled a number on it. "Sammy, call me if I can help you with anything."

Oh, hell, no. What a bitch. Time to pull out his dumb Sammy persona. He came in handy sometimes.

He took the number. "Thank you. Are you in the mosquito killing business?"

Alexandria sucked in her already hollow cheeks. "I don't understand."

"I figured you must have heard I need somebody to spray

the concert site for mosquitoes. Isn't that what you're doing here? That's about all I need."

"Uh, no. I am a pharmaceutical sales rep," she said proudly.

"Oh. Well. Too bad." He reached down and took Pam's hand. "If I have any pharmaceuticals that need repping, I'll be sure to give you a call."

"Uh. Yes." And she left in a tornado of perfume.

Sammy smiled at Pam and she smiled back, but it wasn't the same kind of smile. It was a little sad, and he didn't understand that.

"Why, Sammy?"

"Why what?" He sat down again.

"Why did you do that, and why are you giving me the rush when you could have a girl like Alexandria? I'm nobody special. I'm short and fat and I'm not glamorous like all those women you must meet when you're on the road with Jackson. I haven't achieved anything. I'm uneducated and ill-equipped to run the volunteer project I've taken on. I know I'm convenient, but there are plenty of women who would make themselves convenient for you."

Oh, he hated this. He had to answer, and it could go so wrong, so fast. She was itching to be out of here. He could feel it. And it hurt his heart to know why. She really didn't think she was worth having.

But at least he knew where to start. That was easy.

"First off, you're not fat. And I like short." Those were gimmes. Now it would get hard. "I don't know from glamour, but I do know those women I meet on the road just want a piece of Jackson any way they can get it, and believe me, they aren't getting him. So Chase, the rhythm guitarist, and I seem to be the prime candidates. But that's neither here nor there." He reached for her hand again. "I wasn't lying. I couldn't get you off my mind. I'm just hoping I can keep you from finding out that I'm no prize."

"Ha!" she said. "You have no idea. None."

Seems like he hadn't ruined things, so he was going to quit while he was ahead.

He stood and held out his hand. "Let's go. We have a necking date in my truck down the block from your house."

To his relief, she laughed and took his hand. "Down the block?"

"Did you think I was going to pull right in your driveway?"

~

Ten minutes later, Sammy rolled down his window partway and cut the engine. When he held out his arms, Pam came into them eagerly, though what she whispered in his ear belied that. "I might regret this."

"I'm going to see to it that you don't."

And he did just that.

CHAPTER 8

Pam's head pounded as she walked toward Reed's Jewelry where she was meeting Audrey to help her make bridal selections. She hadn't seen much of Audrey in the three weeks that Sammy had been in town, and in the time they had spent together, Pam had monopolized the conversations, telling and retelling her friend about what was going on with her and Sammy. She felt little guilty about that. After all, she was going to be the maid of honor in Audrey and Max's fall wedding, and she ought to be helping more. And she would when all this was over—the football camp, Sophie's Ann's bedroom, the concert, and Sammy.

Sammy, indeed.

She paused to rub her temple. There were two reasons for her pounding head: Sophie Ann's disastrous color scheme and the longing that Sammy left in her soul and body. And to be honest, she was more concerned about her body than her soul at the moment.

It had been a mistake to take breakfast to Sammy this morning before work. She'd been hungry for him ever since that first kiss, and it seemed he was hungry for her, too. But he'd been true to his word and had not pressed her for sex. Though they did plenty of other things—wonderful things that left them trembling and needing—she had not been able to take the final plunge. After three weeks of bodies-entangled necking and outside-the-clothes stroking, for the first time this morning, Sammy had reached under her shirt and cupped her lace-covered breasts. "Please?" He'd worked his hands to the clasp on her bra. "Can I? I need …" She'd given him the go ahead, and what had followed had been so good and so different from any past experience. He'd lifted, stroked, and teased her nipples until she and Sammy writhed against each other, needing and desperate. Another few pelvic strokes and she would have come—so she'd stopped. But, as ever, he'd been so sweet, so patient, and kind. She wanted to, but she knew what it would mean to her and how much harder it would be when the concert was over and they went their separate ways. And that was bound to happen, wasn't it? Technically, they could have achieved physical satisfaction without completing the act, but she always stopped because she knew the memory of any sort of intimacy, beyond what they'd already done, would be too hard to live with. And he never complained.

At least this little chore would be a distraction.

Audrey stood looking in the store window—though at second glance she wasn't so much looking as she was mesmerized by the round revolving table covered in a white linen cloth and set with six different china, crystal, and silver patterns. A wide pink ribbon separated each place setting. Pam stepped up beside Audrey, and they swapped smiles in a mirror behind the table. Though dressed in her usual athletic attire—Merritt Bobcat blue Under Armour shorts and T-shirt, Audrey was beautiful—thin, blond, tan, and fit. It didn't hurt that she was drop-dead in love.

"It's not every day you see a merry-go-round in a store window," Audrey said.

"That table has been going around and around all my life," Pam said. "Sometimes it has jewelry, sometimes china."

"Did you ever think you might want to sit on it and ride?" Audrey asked. "You could wave at everybody who goes by."

"No, I hadn't thought of that," Pam said. "Do you want to do it?"

"It might be more productive than picking dishes. I am really not good at this kind of thing."

"Maybe not," Pam agreed. "But you are a wonderful photographer."

Audrey shrugged. "How are things with you and Sammy?"

"That's all we've talked about for three weeks. Today is about you."

"Don't remind me. Do you suppose I could just close my eyes and pick one of those?" Audrey pointed to the revolving dishes. "Then we'd be done and we could go to lunch."

Pam laughed. "You're going to get wedding gifts. You might as well get what you like."

"That's what Max's mom says. I love her, so I do what she says. She'd be here, but she had a little minor surgery. She's addressing the wedding invitations while she'd laid up. So I really appreciate your help."

"Maybe it'll make me feel better about myself. I've just come from Sophie Ann's. The painters are done, and I needed to take delivery on the pieces of furniture I sent to be reupholstered."

Audrey made a face. "Is it as bad as you expected?"

"Worse. But Annelle and Lucy know it's not my fault. Either of them would have just refused to do it, but I don't have that luxury. I'm not in charge."

"You can be in charge of my china. I wish someone could

just go inside my head and pick something I would like. Max doesn't care. He said as long as I'm happy, he is. But the thought of looking at forty-seven plates makes my head spin. You know I have no style."

"That's not true." Audrey had grown up in poverty with a drug addict mother. She'd gone to college on a softball scholarship and later become a sportscaster. While at ESPN, an accident had damaged her vocal cords and robbed her of her sportscaster voice. Now she was a budding sports photographer. Audrey's style might still be a work in progress, but Pam could see in her photographs that she was on the way to loving simple, clean lines with no fuss. Pam laid a hand on her arm. "I think we can arrange it so you don't have to look at forty-seven of anything. I might have some ideas."

"Do you think it will take long?" Audrey asked. "Those boys are arriving for the football camp, and I've got to help set up for the cookout tonight."

"We'll be as fast as we can. So Missy has pressed you into service?"

"Me and the rest of the world. You're coming, aren't you?"

"Yes." The question was, would she be dateless? Sammy had said he needed to meet her there because he had to go to Birmingham. Some of Gabe Beauford's former teammates from San Antonio were flying in for the camp, and Sammy had to pick them up. It seemed that Sammy expected for the two of them to be together at the cookout, but if a Beauford needed him, she wasn't sure she'd make the cut.

Audrey looked at the door of the shop and sighed. "I suppose we'd better go in. It's time for my appointment."

The owner, Asa Reed, impeccably dressed with every snowy hair in place, met them at the door.

"If it's not my favorite bride." Mr. Reed was the kind of man who wore seersucker suits in the summer and bow ties and French cuffs year round. "And how are you today, Pam? Is Annelle keeping you busy?"

Actually, Mr. Reed, it's Sammy Anderson who is keeping me busy these days. Maybe you've seen him around with me. We're together all the time, but I have no idea if people think we are a couple or are just working on the concert. Probably the latter. Anyway, he's tall, built, sweet, with the look of a Greek God. I'm busy trying to figure him out, busy rolling around with him in bed, tangled together hip to hip, with his hands inside my bra, busy trying to figure out what's next.

Her nipples prickled at the thought, and Mr. Reed looked at her so strangely that she wondered for a brief second if she had spoken the words that marched through her mind.

"Pam? Dear? Are you all right?"

"Fine. Fine. Just thinking about china!"

"Then we're all on the same page," Mr. Reed said. "My granddaughter usually helps the brides, but I'm taking care of Audrey myself. After all, it's not every day I get a call from a man on Easter Sunday to open up in order to sell him an engagement ring." He laughed. "That boy was in a state. I was right relieved when I heard you'd accepted him, Audrey."

"How could I not?" She looked lovingly at the snowflake-shaped diamond setting on her left hand.

He clapped his hands together. "Well, Audrey, this is how it works. You'll make your selections, and we'll do an order so we'll have plenty in stock when people start buying your wedding gifts. And you'll get a lot of gifts."

"I will?"

She would. Not only was Max Buchanan a renowned plastic surgeon, but he was also first cousins with Missy Bragg and the Beauford brothers, which meant old family and old money. Pam was surprised Max hadn't called Sammy to run errands for him. Or maybe he had and she just didn't know about it.

Mr. Reed laughed. "For sure. I've taken the liberty of setting up eight different place settings. Why don't we start by looking at those? Then we'll eliminate what you don't like and add others."

Audrey's eyes glazed over and her mouth formed an O. She tried to pull her collar, but since she wasn't wearing one, she ended up scratching her neck.

Pam laid a hand on the man's arm. "Mr. Reed, it was really nice of you to go to all that trouble, but Audrey is feeling a little overwhelmed."

He nodded sympathetically. "I understand. Most brides like to look at all the possibilities, but we can do this any way you ladies choose."

"I have an idea. Could you set up Lenox Solitaire with Fairfax silver?

He nodded. "A lovely combination. Lenox Solitaire crystal, as well?"

"No. Too predictable. Let's shake it up a little with Baccarat Mille Nuits."

"Ahh! We have a few stems." Asa was a good businessman, and Pam could see the dollar signs in his eyes. Audrey, on the other hand, hadn't a clue.

"What about Christmas china?" Mr. Reed asked.

"Christmas china!" Audrey looked from one of them to the other. "Is that a thing?"

"Just the Lenox Solitaire Snowflake accent plates, I think," Pam said. "You can have too much of a good thing." *Unless it's lying in Sammy Anderson's arms. Stop!* "But didn't I see some Lenox Merry and Bright mugs and Waterford Snowflake Wishes double old fashioneds in here last Christmas?"

Mr. Reed nodded. "Lovely, Pam."

And it would be, though not what she would have chosen. She would have wanted Vintage Jewel china, Lismore crystal, Old Master silver, and Sammy in a morning suit. Maybe a top hat. The image of that made her laugh. No. No top hat. Sammy wasn't built for hats, except baseball caps. Yes. She penciled in that image in her fantasy. Yes. Perfect. She'd be all right with that, too—though she could just imagine what her mother would say.

"Pam? Are you all right?" Audrey touched her cheek.

Great Jehovah, she had gone into her own little Sammy Anderson world and had laughed out loud. She was going crazy, and Audrey and Mr. Reed knew it.

"Sorry." Maybe she could turn this around. "Was just picturing Audrey's place setting."

Mr. Reed nodded, but she doubted if he believed her. Then again, he probably didn't care.

"Why don't you ladies have a seat over here?" He ushered them to a love seat in the bridal department. "There's coffee in the silver pot there on the table. I'll just go get the china set up so Audrey can see it."

"Do you want coffee?" Pam asked.

"No. I don't want coffee. What is wrong with you? Is it this concert?"

"Hardly. Sammy has taken the whole thing over. And why not? He's much more competent at this than I am."

"Ah. Sammy." Audrey nodded like that was the answer to question of the universe.

"He's out at the Avery farm right now with the stage construction crew. You should see him. He knows everything about this—I mean everything." *And you ought to see him without his shirt. The whole world ought to see him without his shirt. It is a sight no one should be deprived of.*

Audrey smiled a knowing smile, though Pam had no idea what she knew. "Have you had sex yet?"

"Audrey!" Pam looked around to make sure no one was listening.

"Because the last time we talked about this, it was no."

Why, why, why had she told her that?

"It's still no, then?" Audrey lost her smile and looked concerned.

"It's still no," Pam whispered.

"Then I know what's wrong with you. I assume he's still waiting for you to give him the go ahead. He's a patient man. That's for sure. Do you wonder what inspires this patience?"

And what if he became impatient? What if he got tired of waiting and took up with someone like Alexandria?

"I don't know, Audrey. I'm handy? Nothing to lose? I know what he says, but who knows."

"Just what does he say, Pam?"

"He said he didn't want to mess things up. It sounds like I made that up, didn't it? Either that, or it's just an excuse to get away from me."

"Oh, Pam." Audrey laid a hand on Pam's wrist and moved it back and forth. "You stupid, stupid girl. He's in love with you, or very nearly."

Pam's heart lifted, even if it couldn't be true. "But this is fast."

"There was a time when I would have agreed with you." Audrey's own romance had progressed quickly. She'd only known Max three months when they'd gotten engaged. "But when you know, you know." Audrey tilted her head and smiled. "And you know, don't you?"

Did she? Of course she did. That's why she wouldn't have sex with him. If she hadn't been in love with him, sex would have been easy, as it had been with her past three partners. Even that loveless sex had made those breakups more painful, though she realized now that pain had been about hurt pride and dashed hopes of the love that *might* have come. But this was different. What she felt for Sammy wasn't the hope of love. It was love. And if he didn't return the feelings, the pain wouldn't be about pride. It would go straight to the heart.

"Can you even imagine what my parents would say?" Sammy wasn't anything close to what they thought it would take to ease the shame of Pam's failures.

"Listen, Pam—"

"Ladies!" Mr. Reed appeared and clapped his hands together. "I've got it all set up, and I think you're going to be pleased."

Audrey threw Pam a frustrated look—maybe because she'd been interrupted, maybe because she had no patience with china.

But that all changed when Mr. Reed led them to the table where he had laid out the place setting. He'd used pale blue linens, and it was just as lovely as Pam had expected.

Apparently, Audrey thought so, too. To Pam's surprise, she put her hands on her cheeks and gave out a little cry. "It's wonderful! I didn't know. Oh. They are so perfect. Pam, you always know what I like. Even when I don't."

"Good! Good! So happy you like it," Mr. Reed said.

"And see here?" Pam reached for one of the snowflake plates. "This matches the china so you can mix it for just a little Christmas whimsy." Then she set the snowflake plate beside the mug and double old fashioned. "Or you can use these plates for dessert and coffee or party snacks and drinks."

"Oh! And it's snowflakes! Like my ring!"

Joy surged through Pam at seeing her friend so happy. "That was the idea."

And the three of them laughed together.

"Any changes at all?" Mr. Reed asked.

"It's perfect just the way it is."

When Pam and Audrey stepped on the street, Audrey took Pam's arm. "You just did for me what I couldn't figure out for myself. Now, listen to me and let me return the favor about something *I* know about. Let that man love you. It may seem fast, but it's time. And it's time for sex. Come to that cookout tonight loaded for bear and make it happen. I know what I'm talking about."

"I'll think about it." How could she think of anything else?

CHAPTER 9

There was a knock at the pool house door. "Gabe! I'm surprised it's you," Sammy said.

"You knew I was coming—you had me bring you this." He held up a package wrapped in pink tissue paper and tied with a satin ribbon. That would be the handmade lace shawl Sammy had bought for Pam. He'd thought and thought before he'd figured out the perfect gift. He'd wanted something special and unique, like her. He'd run through all the handmade things available in Beauford—Noel's quilts, Heath's stained glass, Neyland's jewelry, and on and on. None of it seemed right until he thought of Helene-Louise's lace. She had helped him decide on the shawl.

"Why are you surprised?"

Sammy took the package and stood aside for Gabe to come in. "I'm surprised because you have never knocked on a door in your life. You barge right in like it's your due to be wherever you want to be."

"Yeah, well." Gabe went to be mini fridge and got a beer. "Considering the nature of that gift, I was afraid of who you might have in here. Didn't want to interrupt anything."

There had been plenty to interrupt, just not exactly what Gabe was thinking. But it was coming. He had to believe that. That girl was driving him insane. And he'd gotten this crazy idea in his head that he *had* to have her in that barn. He'd even made some preparations.

"You want a beer?" Gabe asked.

"You mean do I want one of *my* beers? No. I have to drive to the airport to get your friends. Remember?"

Gabe headed to the sofa, but Sammy headed him off. "Sit in the chair. It's more comfortable." Truth was, he didn't want Gabe to sit where he'd taken Pam's bra off this morning. It seemed wrong.

"Why, thank you, Sammy. I don't believe you have ever been concerned about my comfort before. Do you have anything to eat?"

"No." Sammy laid the package on the table and settled on the couch. He knew Gabe would want food because he always wanted food, but he also knew there was plenty to eat just a few steps away in Missy's kitchen. "When did you get here?"

"This morning. Hours ago. I was going to come out to the concert site to see you, but I fell asleep."

"So you're staying with Missy?"

He nodded. "All week. Plus four of my teammates—present and former. At least the food will be good."

"Do you think of anything except food?"

"Of course I do. Beer. Dr. Pepper. Football. My wife." His voice went soft, though Sammy doubted Gabe knew it. "How are things going here?"

"From what I hear, the football camp is all set."

"I wouldn't expect any less. Nathan Scott's a good man."

"The stage is nearly ready. Everything with the concert is on track, too."

"I wouldn't expect any less. You're a good man."

"Just doing my job. Thanks for picking that up for me." Sammy gestured to the pink package on the table.

"You'd better unwrap it to make sure I got the right one."

Sammy looked at the ribbon doubtfully. "Helene-Louise did a nice wrapping job. I'll never be able to put it back together like this."

"You can put it in a gift bag. I risked my life to get that. I'd hate it if it's wrong."

Reluctantly Sammy untied the ribbon. "Risked your life?"

"Do you remember when Neyland first opened Sparkle? Not in the place where it is now, but the place she had to give up because her jewelry wasn't selling."

"Yeah. I guess I remember something about that."

"She had hoped to make enough money to reopen in the same location, but here comes Helene-Louise Soileau who rented the space for her lace making shop. That was when I was trying to court Neyland. I promised her I would never buy anything made of lace. I might have even called Helene-Louise a vile weaver of webs and promised try to get lace outlawed in this country."

Sammy's ears perked up. "Did it work?"

Gabe took a sip of his beer. "Did what work?"

"Making that promise to Neyland?"

Gabe shrugged. "Who knows? There was so much that worked and didn't work back then, that I can't sort it out. Since Neyland's got a new Sparkle and is doing well, I like to think it wouldn't matter to her, but I still wouldn't want her to know I've been buying stuff from Helene-Louise."

"Technically, you didn't. I did. You were just the errand boy."

"Don't count on Neyland seeing it that way. Or any woman. Sammy, never count on thinking you know what a woman is going to do. It will sink you in quicksand every single time."

Truer words had never been spoken.

"Finish opening that package. When you pay a thousand dollars for a piece of lace, it needs to be the right one."

"It's worth a thousand dollars. It's silk, and it took Helene-Louise hours and hours to make it." And it would be worth a hundred times that if Pam liked it. "Maybe Missy has a gift bag she can give me." But it wasn't a bad idea to get a look at it before he gave it to Pam. He and Helene-Louise had texted for two hours, with her sending him pictures until he picked the best one. He unfolded the layers of paper, held up the shawl, and nodded with satisfaction. It was something called bobbin lace. "This is the one."

"I don't really understand that gift, Sammy. You could have gotten some really nice lace underwear for half what that cost. Women like that. And you would, too."

The thought made Sammy cringe. "Not this woman. She would be embarrassed. She's classy. And special—way too special for me, but she might not know that, and I don't plan on pointing it out."

Gabe sucked in his breath and let out a low whistle. "Oh, Lord in heaven, Sammy. You're way too young for this. How old are you? Twenty-six?"

"Twenty-four."

"See? At twenty-four, I was sowing oats so deep that they still haven't come up."

At twenty-four, Gabe had had a Heisman trophy and a first round draft pick under his belt. And he'd been about to win his first Super Bowl. Sammy didn't care about any of that. He only wanted keep doing what he was doing and win Pam.

"It happens when it happens." Sammy ran his fingers over the shawl. Soft. Delicate.

"But a shawl? Why a shawl? Is she Amish? Or a pioneer?"

Sammy shook his head. "Episcopalian. I wanted to get her something nice."

Gabe crossed his ankle over his knee. "Well, you sure did. You could have gotten her a churn way cheaper."

"I don't believe she does much churning. Besides, I can afford it. Your brother pays me plenty. Treats me like family."

"I didn't say you couldn't afford it. And you *are* family. I just think it's a little early for you to be buying shawls."

"Better early than late." Sammy stood up. "Speaking of late, I need to go to the airport if I want to be on time for the cookout. And I do."

Gabe stood, too. "When am I going to meet this classy, special, too-good-for-you woman, this wonder chick?"

"At the cookout tonight. And don't call her wonder chick."

"You *have* got it bad. God be with you. I've been there. Still am." Gabe picked up the shawl and the wrappings. "I'll get Missy to put this back together for you."

"Thanks. Just leave it there on the table."

"I hope you know what you're doing, Sammy."

"Hope hard, because I probably don't."

CHAPTER 10

"Missy and Caroline really did it up right, didn't they?" Tiptoe greeted Pam as she walked through the practice field where the cookout was being held.

"What in the world? I didn't expect all these tents. I thought this was going to be a few grills, picnic tables, and coolers full of soft drinks."

There was a hamburger, hotdog, and bratwurst bar with every gourmet condiment you could think of, numerous bowls of cold salads, towers of cupcakes and cookies, and an ice cream sundae station. Under a small red-striped tent there was what looked like an old fashioned soda fountain where Harris Bragg, Max Buchanan, and Luke Avery were serving iced tea and soft drinks. And that was just the food. There was a band playing and a portable dance floor.

"This looks more like an upscale society party than hamburgers and hotdogs for high school football players."

Tiptoe laughed. "Well, there are the parents and all those pro football players Missy brought in. You know Missy and Caroline. They don't want anyone to think Merritt would put on a tacky party."

Pam spotted Miss Caroline drifting through the crowd touching arms and bestowing smiles. As for Missy, she was under the tent where the Rotary was grilling meat, with a clipboard under her arm and an instant read thermometer in her hand. She'd evidently found something lacking, because she grabbed Brantley Kincaid by the arm, hauled him to the side of the tent, and began pointing and ranting—at which time he also began pointing and ranting.

"Looks like business as usual with those two," Pam said.

Tiptoe laughed. "They've been like that all their lives. Are you here alone tonight?"

"No she's not," came a voice behind her. An arm went around her shoulders as Sammy stepped up and extended his other hand to Tiptoe. "How're you doing, Mr. Tiptoe?"

Sammy was making it clear—right here in public—that they were each other's dates. While they had been seen together around town plenty of times, it had mostly been when they were grabbing a quick meal or running a concert-related errand. She hadn't given it much thought, but this was different—and it felt good.

"Mighty fine, Sammy. Mighty fine." Tiptoe let his eyes rest on the arm around Pam's shoulders. "Looks like you're doing fine yourself."

"I am." And Sammy smiled at Pam like he meant it. Would people be wondering what on earth Sammy saw in someone like her? Were they already?

Tiptoe tipped an invisible hat. "I'll leave you two to it. Don't get in trouble. I hear we've got a storm brewing. Let's hope we can get these kids fed before it hits—though I'm sure Missy has an alternate plan."

Sammy turned Pam to face him. "You look pretty. I like your little skirt and shirt." But he wasn't looking at her plain knee-length khaki skirt and white knit V-neck. He was looking at her breasts. She giggled and he raised his gaze to hers, half closed his eyes, and tossed his head.

"You caught me," he said.

Her breath caught at this morning's memory.

Sammy ran his hands up her arms, and the mood changed from light and humorous to heavy and poignant. He ran his thumb over her lower lip.

"There's a great day coming, Pam Carson. And I will be there."

Maybe that day had come. She drew a ragged breath.

He put his hands on her shoulders. "I'm glad to see you."

"How was your trip to the airport?" Why had she even asked that?

He gave out a little laugh. "Fine. But I knew it would be." He winked. "I'm an expert at airport pickup. You can only get so good at it, and I am as good as anyone is ever going to be. If you ever need an airport pickup, I'm your guy."

But are you my guy in other ways? All ways? It seems like you want me to think that's true, but is it?

"I'll keep that in mind."

He ran a finger down her cheek. "I've got a present for you. I was going to wait until later to give it to you, but I want you to have it now."

He looked excited—like an eight-year-old at his birthday party where he was just sure there was going to be a Red Ryder BB gun. It was the most endearing moment of her life.

"Did you buy this gift at the airport?"

He looked appalled. "No. I did *not* buy it at the airport. What did you think? That I saw one of those giant triangle-shaped candy bars and thought, "Well, that's just what I've been wanting to get for my girl?"

His girl. She risked a little bit of herself and laid a hand on his cheek. "I would have loved it because you thought of me."

His eyes went all soft and shiny at the same time. "Then

you're really going to like this. " He let go of her shoulders and took her arm. "It's in my truck. Why don't we go get it? Then we can come back and eat?"

"You've got me curious." *And happy. Please let me continue to be happy.*

"I'm parked on the other side." And he wove his fingers through hers until they were palm to palm and began to guide her through the crowd. It was not a fast journey. Spirits were high, and everyone wanted to talk to everyone else. No doubt some of them wanted to feast on Sammy's good looks and wonder how Pam had gotten him to hold her hand. It was a wonder they made it past the Junior League dessert tent with all his clothes still intact.

Pam floated through it all, vaguely aware that Nathan Scott had been on a tear about Missy ignoring his team nutrition plan when drawing up the menu, Mary Nell Adcock had thought there would be wine, and Arabelle Garrett had to perform the Heimlich maneuver on a brawny sixteen-year-old whose hotdog had gone down all wrong.

Pam continued to float when Audrey stopped serving Coca-Cola cake long enough to hum a few bars of "Tonight's the Night" and when Sammy introduced her to Gabe Beauford and some football players who she was maybe supposed to be impressed with but wasn't. It was hard to be impressed with anything except the man beside her holding her hand.

No doubt about it. She was approaching that dangerous place of embracing the level of happy that might produce a memory that would break her heart and make the rest of her life hard to live.

"Finally," Sammy said when they stood on the still-hot asphalt of the parking lot between Sammy's truck and an SUV, with the smell of grilling meat in the air and laughter from the crowd in the background. The homegrown band did a bad rendition of "Must Be Doing Something Right."

Pam thought he would kiss her, wanted him to kiss her, but instead he reached into the truck and brought out a small package.

"Open it."

She untied the white satin ribbon and unfolded the heart-scattered pink tissue paper. "This paper is handmade."

"Yeah? Glad I didn't throw it away then. I unwrapped it, but Gabe had Missy fix it back for me."

It was lace, but what? The package had been so small that Pam was amazed when it continued and continued to unfold until she held a gossamer shawl, so light and ethereal that it must have been made by fairies—and it had to be fairy magic that was creating the feeling inside her. She would always have this. Even when—no *if*, it had to be if—she never saw Sammy after the concert, she'd have this evidence that he'd thought of her.

She brought the lace to her cheek. Silk. No doubt about it. "Sammy, I've never had—never seen—anything this beautiful. I don't know what to say."

"Just say you'll wear it." He took it and drew it around her shoulders. "Don't save it for 'good.' My grandmother died with a drawer full of things she'd saved for good."

"I promise." Pam folded the paper she still held. She would save that, would line a drawer with it. "Where did you get such a lovely thing?"

"Beauford. You know the whole town is full of those fancy artists that people come from all over to buy from. Helene-Louise Soileau. She makes lace. She has two apprentices, but she made this one herself," he said proudly.

Pam ran her hand over the lace. "She sounds French."

"Not really. She's from New Orleans, and she talks just like the rest of us." Then he laughed to show he was making a joke, and she joined in. Just then the band shifted into

"Tonight's the Night," and Pam laughed harder and wondered how much Audrey had tipped them.

Sammy looked back toward the crowd. "So do you want to go get some food? Maybe dance? I'm a pretty good dancer."

She opened her mouth to say yes, because she always said yes—except to the one thing she really wanted. And, indeed, tonight was the night. Fairy magic had put her over the edge.

"No." She slowly put her arms around Sammy's neck, pulled his mouth to hers, and kissed him for all she was worth. He stiffened with surprise, and she understood why. She had never once initiated a kiss with him, had always been too afraid he'd rebuff her. But it only took a split second for him to recover and respond, encircling her in his arms and holding her tight. She ran her fingers over the back of his neck, and he shuddered, like he always did. She thought she heard thunder in the distance, but she wasn't sure if it was real or in her head.

He lightly bit her bottom lip and drew her tongue deeper into his mouth. Their pelvises were inches apart, and she knew if she pressed against him she'd find him hard. She was right, so right, but he lengthened still more. He was too tall for it to fit where her thighs met, but she moved against him anyway, enjoying the moment. He let a hand drop to her bottom and brought her closer in still.

She couldn't get her breath, and if she didn't breathe she might pass out.

She broke the kiss.

His mouth was barely a half-inch from hers when he said, "I swear you are music in my head. So no food?"

"No food." And she did something she had not done before. She reached between them and stroked the length of his penis.

His knees almost most buckled. "Thor's thunder, woman. You are *killing* me."

"No food," she repeated. "All I want is you—all of you this time. Not a half grope, ending in wanting and frustration. I want you. It's time. I'm saying so." And she continued to stroke.

He pulled her hand away and led her quickly—very quickly, indeed—to the passenger side of the truck. He jerked open the door and lifted her inside, pausing only to grind against her one more time and kiss her mouth hard and quick.

"I'm getting you out of here before you change your mind."

"I won't change my mind." And even if she'd wanted to, her pulsating genitals wouldn't have let her.

CHAPTER 11

Sammy might have pulled up her skirt and taken her right against his truck if the voice inside him hadn't shouted, "Don't mess this up!" He'd always been one and done kind of guy. Not that he hadn't had compliments and plenty of women who'd wanted another round—but it was usually satisfy her, satisfy himself, and get on with life. This had to be different.

When he turned onto the road that would take them out of town, Pam said, "Where are we going?" Her voice was a little tight and squeaky.

"The Avery farm."

"The Avery farm? But I thought …"

"You thought right. We just aren't going to the pool house." He reached over and slid his hand up her skirt and squeezed the inside of her thigh. He'd never touched her bare flesh there before. And this was just the beginning. "Laugh if you want. But the first night that I kissed you, when I said I wanted to take you in that barn—do you remember?"

She laughed a little. "Oh, I remember. I assure you I remember."

"Well, I can't get it off my mind—you, me, and that barn loft. Trust me."

She nodded, big-eyed. "Will there be hay up there? I haven't been in the loft."

"No. The Averys don't keep animals."

"I thought all barns had hay." She pulled the shawl tighter around her.

"I would not make love to you in a pile of hay. It's dirty, buggy, and sometimes there are snakes. No. No hay and no sand. That's only a good idea in movies."

"Sounds like you speak from experience."

"I speak from experience of *not* doing it under those conditions. I have pretty good common sense." He pulled up beside the barn that was about to go down in history. He gave her thigh a final squeeze, unbuckled her seatbelt, and pulled her hard against him. "You need to stay in the truck for a minute while I get everything fixed."

She nodded with a puzzled look and, lifting her face, parted her pretty little mouth.

He jerked back. "No! Do not kiss me, Pam. If you do, I swear, I'll pull you astride me and have you right now. And I don't want it to be like that for you." He paused. "At least not the first time. Maybe later. Actually, that sounds pretty good." Thunder rumbled, interrupting the fantasy of that.

He jumped out of the truck, opened the rear door, and pulled out the canvas bag he'd put there.

"What's that?" Pam asked.

"My bag of hope. Sit tight. I'll be right back."

~

*P*am popped an Altoid, combed her hair, and refused to think while Sammy was gone—if she did, she might run. She'd remembered too late that he was going to see her naked. At least the barn was dark. Or she hoped it would be. Even with all her comings and goings, she hadn't been in there since her class had built their home-coming float. But wait. They'd built it at night. There were lights. Oh, damn. She should have never come.

Because more than all that, she was about to do what she'd never come back from. But she was sunk anyway. Truth be told, Sammy's sweet words and hints of their future had sunk her a long time ago. What he seemed to be offering was like an antique china teacup—lovely, but fragile. It could shatter so easily right in her hands. But there was no running from what was about to happen with Sammy.

It was too late to run now anyway, even if she'd had her car, even if the Averys had a tractor she could steal, because Sammy was jerking the truck door open and hauling her out by her hand.

"All set. Hurry." Heavy, fat raindrops fell as he pulled her after him. "The bottom is fixing to drop out."

And it did—just as they reached shelter. Lightning flashed, thunder boomed, and raindrops became sheets.

Sammy turned her toward him and smiled a pleased-with-himself smile—which she could see because he'd turned on the small light over the door.

"Do you think it's a good idea to have the light on?" she asked hopefully. "What if Luke and Lanie see the light on the way home from the cookout and investigate?"

Sammy smiled and smoothed her hair. "They won't. Even if they drove all the way down here, which they won't, they know my truck. They would assume I'm here doing some-thing. Which I am. Or am about to be. We need the light to climb the ladder to the loft." He led her toward the ladder. "You go first so I can catch you if you slip."

"When my class built our float, we weren't supposed to go to the loft except to get supplies. The chaperone was always going up there to make sure kids weren't up to no good. But some were anyway." She was babbling—about sex. What could be worse?

He laughed low and sweet. "How about you, Pam? Did you get up to no good?" He stroked her bottom as she climbed.

"No. Not then. Later. But I don't want to talk about it. But in case you wondered if I had never done it …"

By now they were at the top of the ladder. He took her in his arms. "I hadn't wondered. It's none of my business. All that's my business is here and now."

Then he turned her toward the center of the loft. She could not believe what she saw—there was a mattress covered in a sheet and a blanket, and two pillar candles with flickering wicks caused by the fan he'd set up in front of the large loft window.

"You planned this." The candles were a bit misshapen.

"I hoped. I told you it was the bag of hope, though those candles do look kind of hopeless. They didn't mix too well with the heat." He grinned. If she had ever wondered about the true definition of adorable, that was it.

"You could not have had that mattress in that bag. Was it here?" Maybe it was from some recent float building.

"No. I bought it and snuck up here at night. It's new."

If she'd ever wondered about romance, this was it.

"You did all this for me?"

He nodded. "Well, for me, too. But the sheets and candles —for you. I didn't need that." He stroked her face. "Come to think of it, it's all for you. I only need you."

Then his mouth was hers and he molded her body to his. The time was here. It was going to happen.

He led her to the mattress and eased her down. "I'm going to undress you now."

She started to warn him that she was fat, but maybe if she didn't say it, he wouldn't notice.

He unwrapped the shawl that she still wore, folded it, and laid it aside.

She stopped him when he reached for her shirt. "No. Now you. It's only fair."

"Fair? Hmm. *You* take off my shirt. That's fair."

She undid the buttons and pushed it off his shoulders. She'd seen him shirtless once when she'd come out to check on the stage and he'd been hauling wood from a truck—but that had been at a distance. When he'd caught sight of her, he'd put on his T-shirt as he walked toward her. The sight had been fine enough, but here, up close, he was a work of art and one she couldn't believe she was going to be allowed to touch.

"You work out," she said.

He shrugged. "Come here. Can we dispense with fair and just get naked? Really fast? I can't get you close enough."

And that's how it happened that in less than a minute, they were skin to skin, her breasts against his chest, their mouths melded—but the undressing was the last thing that happened fast.

He laid her back and ran his hands over her hips, thighs, and breasts as the fan washed cool, rain-scented air over them.

"You're beautiful," he said. "I don't think you know that. I didn't know it either. All my life, people have pointed to sharp-hipped, mean-looking women and said they were beautiful. I've just always thought, 'Okay. I don't like beautiful. I like cute.' But that's wrong. I just now understand. They don't know beautiful. They are entitled to their opinion I guess, but you are my kind of beautiful."

This had to be a dream. He meant it. This man, who

turned heads when he walked down the street, really believed she was beautiful.

"You are so lush." He cupped her breasts. "The first day I saw you, your sweater was too big, and I saw your breasts when you bent over."

Oh, hell. "No! Oh, no."

"Yes. It's all I could think about for three months. I'd dream of them and wake up with aching balls. Here. Let me."

He bent and teased first one nipple and then the other with his lips, then suckled lightly until she pulled his head in.

"Harder? Do you want it harder?" His voice was raspy.

"Yes. Please. Oh. That's right."

And he knew just what to do, just like she could tell sometimes what people were thinking. He bit lightly and sucked until they were both trembling and moaning.

The flesh between her thighs throbbed and twitched with each pull of his mouth.

When she finally reached to stroke his penis, as hard as diamonds, it jerked in her hand and he moaned.

"Lightly, sweetheart," he said. "Any more and I'll come." His fingers replaced his mouth on her nipples and he kissed his way up her neck to the sensitive spot below her ear. "Before you were ready—before you asked—I could have satisfied you, we could have satisfied each other."

"You were never mad when I stopped."

"No. I didn't want to come in my pants like some teenager on a back road—though I came close. I wanted for us to come like a man and woman with me inside you and you all around me." He rolled until his penis was between her thighs, barley touching, very close to torture. "And I didn't want you to say yes in the heat of the moment because you wanted sex. I wanted you to say yes because you wanted *me.*"

"I do," she said. "So please do it."

"Are you sure? Sure you're ready? Sure you're wet?" He

stroked her and she pressed against his hand. "I guess that answers that."

She sat up and stroked his inner thighs as he, grinning into her eyes, rolled the condom on. She slid a hand down and cupped his balls.

He closed his eyes. "Yes. Do that. Just a little." He seemed paralyzed in the moment, but then, he stretched like a cat and pushed her against the mattress. "There is so much I want to do to you, so much I want you to do to me. But for now, it has to be this." He knelt between her legs. "Put your hands on me, Pam. Guide me inside you."

She reveled in the heat of him against her palms and tipped her hips until his throbbing fullness met her opening.

He moaned. "I'll take it from here." He settled into her until he was fully sheathed, and she instinctively raised her legs to draw him in farther.

It was as though they had been made for each other.

"Perfect," he whispered, placing a hand on her thigh to bring her closer. "I'm very deep. Is it too much?"

"Perfect," she echoed, bucking against him. "So perfect."

He stilled her with a squeeze to her thigh. "Not yet. Lie still. Let me feel you. Feel me. Waiting has been hell. Let's appreciate every bit of heaven."

And it was heaven, feeling the bond with the only movement the involuntary twitching of his penis inside her. He raised himself with one arm and looked at her in the candlelight. "It *is* different." It seemed he was almost talking to himself. He kissed her long and deep, and the tension built until she could stand it no longer.

"Sammy." She squirmed against him. "I need ... I have to move."

He clamped down hard. "Long, slow strokes." He cupped her bottom to guide her though one, two, three strokes. Then he loosened his hips.

"Again," she begged.

And he went deep and held again. "Go slow. Slow and hard."

"Don't stop!" And she rolled her hips until the spasms came, long, hard, and endless. She couldn't stop the sounds that she made, wouldn't have if she could have when she saw how delighted he was with her—and himself.

"Good?" He stared down at her.

"You don't know. But I want you to feel it, too." She lifted her hips again. "How about something special for you?"

"In time, in time." And he lifted his body, lightly teasing her with his pubic ridge until she fell down that black hole of desire again. Soon, she was begging for more, and he gave it to her, gave her everything she wanted until he brought her home twice more.

When he would have tried for a fourth, she placed his hands on his hips. "No more. I can't stand any more."

"Ever?"

"For now." Because there had to be more after this, had to. "Are you ready?"

"Oh, baby." He began to move inside her with abandon. "So ready. So close."

His face was a study in pleasure and pain and everything in between. When she met his hard strokes, he bit his lip; when she ran her hands up his sides, he cried out; when she reached to stroke his balls, he buried his head in her neck and made primal sounds.

He built and built, and for all that she had not been able to read him as she read other people, she knew without question when the moment was imminent, and she knew what he wanted.

She lifted her hips high, grabbed his bottom, and pulled him in deeper still. He cried out and rolled his hips against her and—just as his spasms jolted inside her, the words he cried out jolted her heart:

"I love you, Pam. I love you! You don't even know."

Even if they were only words spoken in passion, it was a memory she would save.

He collapsed on her, damp with sweat, and panting. They lay still for some minutes before he rolled off her.

"Sorry. I know I'm crushing you."

"Crush on." She held her arms out to him. It was a small price to pay for the closeness.

Smiling, he raised himself to a sitting position and pulled her onto his lap. "I just need a few minutes." He reached into his hope bag and brought out a small, soft-sided cooler.

"A few minutes?"

"You don't really imagine that we're done for the night, do you? Like I said, I've got a whole list of stuff I want to do to you—starting with my mouth right here." He ran his hand over her crotch and—though she could scarcely believe it—she began to warm there again. How was that even possible this soon, as satisfied as he'd left her? But the stirring was there.

He held a cold bottle of water to her lips. "Thirsty?"

She laughed. "You have cold water in your hope bag?"

He showed his perfect teeth when he smiled—teeth that had aroused her and would again. "I was very hopeful. I have put in a fresh bottle every day that God has sent for nearly three weeks. Didn't think about the candles."

"How much longer would you have done it?"

He looked serious. "As long as I had to." He took a drink from the bottle and gave another to her. Then he reached for the shawl and draped it over her head.

"What? What are you doing?" The lace tickled her face and she brushed it back.

"I'm going to want to see you like this some day, you know. Walking toward me."

Her gut twisted. "What?" she said lightly. "Naked? With a shawl on my head?" Her heart pounded at the insinuation.

"I'll take that. But walking toward me with lace on your head."

She didn't know what to say, but it didn't matter. He kissed her with sweetness, passion, and all encompassing wholeness—though she wasn't sure that made sense. But she was sure that it was the most romantic kiss of her life.

When he drew back, there was an evil little glint in his eyes. He glazed her nipples with the lace, tickling them to erect points and sending electric currents to her core.

"Lay back," Sammy commanded. He let the soft lace drift down her chest, over her stomach, and around her thighs. Who knew something so light and feathery could be so arousing and so sensuous?

"Not between my legs," she said heavily. "Don't ruin it. Though the idea is interesting."

He laughed a happy laugh. "That's fair." He rubbed it against her breasts and she moaned. "Am I making you want me again?"

"Oh, yes. But I'm so lazy, I can't move. I can't return the favor."

"I don't want you to yet. I want to do this. You make me want you just by being. But my turn will come. And you'll make me *desperate* for you."

She half opened one eye and smiled at him. He laid the shawl aside and picked up the cold water bottle. To her surprise, he rolled it against one nipple and then the other.

"I thought you were going to drink!"

"I am." Then he poured a droplet of water on her nipple and lapped it up with his tongue—the wet cold followed by the wet warm was painfully wonderful.

"The other one. Do the other nipple," she demanded.

"That's right, baby. Tell me what you want. Always tell me what you want." He ministered to her nipples time and time again and then began sprinkling droplets down her torso, lapping as he went. As he dipped lower and lower, she became more and more eager. She knew what was coming, and it was going to be life-changing good.

Drops on her belly, then on top of her thighs, and on the inside of her thighs. And just when she thought she could predict what was next and spread her legs to make herself more accessible, he surprised her by rolling the frosty bottle up the inside of her thigh and upward, teasing her pubic mound.

"Sammy, please. Please."

"Don't have to tell me twice."

She felt the icy water drip against her clitoris and tensed, anticipating Sammy's warm, flicking tongue …

Then like a steel javelin through a cloud, music blared into the quiet, rainy night.

"And I'm stuck out here with a bad sunburn, a surprise tattoo, and a spring break state of mind!"

Pam jerked upward, and Sammy spilled the remaining water on her crotch.

"What? What?" She flailed around. Why was Jackson Beauford singing "Spring Break State of Mind" in the barn loft where they were having sex, for God's sake? At lightning speed, Pam crawled on all fours toward her clothes, as Sammy reached for his pants.

"Fuck, fuck, fucking hell!" he cursed.

But he wasn't reaching for his pants to put them on. He was fishing for his phone.

His *phone*? "Really? You're going to answer the phone? Right *now*?"

"I have to. *If* I ever find it." He grappled with his pants some more. "This is the ring tone for the phone that Jackson uses when he needs me right damn now!" Finally, it appeared in his hand. "Jackson? What in the hell? No. I don't know anything about that. Yes, I have seen Gabriel, and he didn't say a word. Did you think I wouldn't have done it?" He paused, met her eyes, and sighed. "Yes. Yes. I understand. I'll text when I'm headed your way."

What? Headed his way?

"Sure. No. It's okay. Don't worry about that. I'll handle it. See you in a few hours. You're welcome."

But what about me? Pam wanted to cry. She pulled the blanket over her.

"I'm sorry," Sammy said after hanging up. "I've got to go to Beauford Bend. Tonight."

"I gathered." Her voice sounded more clipped that she meant.

"Don't be mad." He came to sit by her and took her hand. "You know Jackson's youngest brother, Beau? He does woodworking. He's apprenticed to Will Garrett, here in Merritt."

"I think I heard that."

"Well, you know Will is odd. And he's very selective about the projects he takes, but he has a commission lined up for Beau. Beau is meeting with the client tomorrow at noon, but there's a book he is supposed to look at before then. Something about studying a certain style of something. Will had the bookstore here in town order it. Anyway, it came in just this morning. Gabe was supposed to pick it up and ask me to drive it up there. But he didn't. So I need to find Bryon Masters and get him to open up and let me have the book so I can take it."

Pam was baffled at how little sense that made. "Why didn't they order it from Amazon? They would have delivered it overnight."

"I don't know." Sammy got up and started to dress.

"Couldn't Beau look up what he needed to know on the Internet? You can find anything on the Internet."

Sammy shook his head as he buttoned his shirt. "I don't know."

"And why can't one of those Beaufords meet you halfway, so you don't have to drive so far tonight?"

"Pam, again, I don't know. It isn't my job to ask to those questions. It's my job to do what is needed of me."

Dressed, he came and sat beside her again. "I'm sorry. Being interrupted at that particular moment wasn't my favorite thing either."

"I don't think Gabe's thoughtlessness and their poor planning constitutes your emergency."

"But it does. If you knew what Jackson pays me, you'd think so, too." He smiled and cupped her face. "Hey! I've got an idea. Let's have an adventure. Come with me. We can get the book and save Beau. Then we can go to my place and finish what we started." He leered at her. "Then we'll get a few of hours of sleep and head back in the morning. You can see where I live. Gwen will feed us breakfast. It'll be fun. Best of all, I can sleep with you and wake up with you."

If anything would have gotten her, that would have been it, but she was tremendously out of sorts and in no mood to get over it. And no wonder. Her genitals had not gotten the message that party time was over.

"What do you say?" Sammy smiled like he knew he was going to get the answer he wanted.

"No." She didn't even consider it, didn't let herself think there could be anything fun or adventurous about it. "I have to go to work tomorrow."

He looked crestfallen. "Oh. Are you sure you couldn't take off? Just half the day? I promise to have you back by noon."

Unless Jackson Beauford wants you to iron his pants or polish his shoes. Then my needs would go completely out the window.

"Can *you* take off *tonight*?" That might not be fair, but the most romantic, significant night of her life had been interrupted because some spoiled rotten people needed an errand run and Sammy was unwilling to tell them no. She wasn't in the mood for fair. Never mind that she had plenty of vacation time and there was nothing pressing at work. Annelle would have given her the whole day off without a second thought.

Sammy nodded. "I see your point." He reached for his hope bag, which seemed more like a hopeless bag now. "Get dressed and I'll pick up here. Then I'll take you to your car."

"All right."

"And, Pam? I'll make this up to you. I promise."

CHAPTER 12

"I can't thank you enough." Sammy took the bag that Byron Masters handed him. After taking Pam to her car at the high school, Sammy had found Bryon in the cafeteria where the cookout had become a cook-in. Byron had agreed without hesitation to unlock the store for Sammy. It's a good thing for Gabe, that Sammy hadn't seen him.

"No problem. Can I get you anything else?"

Sammy shook his head. "Unless you have a book on how to get a mad woman in a good mood again."

Byron shook his head and chuckled. "If such a book existed, it would probably be a bestseller."

No doubt. That's about how his luck was turning out tonight. He took Beau's book and got in his truck that still smelled like Pam—lemony with a little sex mixed in.

She had sat primly and quietly with that shawl folded in her lap all the way back into town. Fearing he'd make things worse, he hadn't said much either. She had allowed him to kiss her goodbye, but she hadn't opened her mouth or her arms. Not that he blamed her for being mad; he wasn't in the best of moods himself. He was hungry, his balls ached, and he was about to have to drive six hours round trip to Beauford Bend—something he could have easily already done today if Gabe had only taken care of what he'd been supposed to this morning.

But those weren't the only sources of his disgruntlement. He'd said the words, the words he'd never said before, and she hadn't said them back. He hadn't let it faze him much at the time. After all, he hadn't meant to tell her he loved her at that precise second. Who could blame her for not responding? A man might say a lot of things he didn't mean at that moment of sweet, sweet relief. But he had meant it, and he'd intended to tell her that after making love to her again—when he wasn't pumping and spilling inside her and he could think straight.

That could have been happening right now, but no. She was mad, and he was driving away from her, horny as hell with no idea how to fix this mess.

But he'd think about it. Given enough time, he could usually figure things out.

~

*P*am awoke abruptly to the sound of angry piano music. Not good. She groaned and sat on the side of the bed. There was no air stirring at all, and she was covered with a fine film of sweat.

If last night hadn't ended badly enough, she'd come home to find that lightning had struck the central air conditioning unit. It's a wonder she'd slept as much as she had, battling the four Hs—hurt, horny, hot, and hungry, in that order.

Yes. Hurt had to come first. Sammy had thought she was mad, and she had been at first. Maybe she still was, a little. But mostly, she was hurt—which was unlike her. She had always worked so hard at being a good sport that she seldom left herself any time to be hurt. But how could she not be? There for just a bit, she'd felt … cherished? Was that the word? And then he'd answered the phone. Who answered the phone at such a time? And then he'd been so eager to do Jackson Beauford's bidding that he hadn't even tried to appease her. Okay, so he had. But he hadn't tried hard enough.

And now her mother was playing that piano, making it sound like it was going to split in two any second—which she always did when she was mad. Truth was, her career as a concert pianist had been an abysmal failure, and she always punished the piano with her fury. Pam wasn't surprised. It didn't take much to make Leslie Carson mad, and a dead air conditioner in this heat was more than enough to do it.

Pam picked up her phone to check the time, half hoping for a text from Sammy. No text. Well, that was fine. Probably for the best. She'd always known she'd have to get over it. Might as well start now.

As for the time—it wasn't even 6 o'clock. She considered taking a shower, but she'd just be sweaty again before it was time to get ready for work. Might as well go try to pour oil on the troubled waters in the music room.

"You're playing early," Pam said mildly as she entered the room.

Leslie stopped playing and whirled around. "There are a lot of reasons for that."

Pam sat on the little needlepoint settee, which was a mistake. The wool threads against her bare thighs didn't do much to improve her comfort.

Pam nodded, but she didn't ask for the grievances on the fury list. Leslie would enumerate them soon enough without prompting.

Leslie began, "It's hot."

"It is that. Too bad the storm knocked out the unit."

"We could have gone to the Merritt Inn if you hadn't filled it up with your football people," Leslie accused.

"I'm sorry." There was no point in defending herself.

"They've had to go to Nashville to get a new unit. We'll be lucky if it's installed before bedtime tonight."

Too bad she hadn't known that. Sammy could have brought it back.

"Then I hope we're lucky."

"Your father went to work early to get out of the heat."

Pam got the idea that her mother was just working up to the main injustice of the day, but maybe she could head it off.

"Why don't you do that, too?" Pam asked. "Go somewhere —out to breakfast and then maybe shopping or to the library or a movie. Get out of the heat. I'm sure the repairman can call when he's ready to come."

"Oh, believe me. I intend to do just that. I'm going to Joyce Tate's house to sit by the pool. But first I need to deal with *you.*"

Oh, hell. Pam remained quiet and waited.

"Joyce called me at 5:30 this morning and invited me as soon as I told her about our disaster."

This was probably not the best time to tell her mother that she might not completely understand the meaning of *disaster.*

Instead she said, "That's early for a phone call."

"Joyce is a good friend, and she wanted to tell me before I heard it from somebody else."

Fingers of dread began to tickle the back of Pam's neck. Still, she said nothing.

"Pam, did you not think I would hear that you've taken up with that handyman? After holding hands with him and leaving before the party even got started?"

Dread stopped tickling and started choking her. Why had she not thought of this?

"I didn't know Joyce was at that cookout," Pam said. "I don't recall seeing her name on the list."

"She wasn't. But her daughter-in-law, Marcia, was. The Blossom Shop is apparently a sponsor of this event."

Well, of course. You could always count on Marcia to spread the word.

"I've always liked Marcia—except when I don't."

"So you don't deny it?" Leslie demanded.

Don't worry, Mother. It was over before it began. The point is moot. I'm not a priority to Sammy. Also, it's easy to want to be with a person who is nice and accommodating all the time, which I was until last night. But she wasn't going there.

"I deny that Sammy is a handyman. He's Jackson Beauford's personal assistant."

Leslie waved her hand. "Handyman. Personal assistant. What difference does it make? You have to stop this now. I have accepted that you don't have any career ambition, that you're content with being a shop girl and running errands for Annelle Mead and Lucy Kincaid, but you cannot align yourself with an errand boy! Someone has to have a real job. I know this Sammy is good-looking—*extraordinarily so.* But this is unacceptable."

Inasmuch as Pam hated to see Sammy kowtowing to the Beaufords, she couldn't stop herself from defending him.

"Sammy has a real job. He works hard. So do I, for that matter."

"That's not what I mean, and you know it. Ditch diggers work hard."

"And a good thing. Where would we be without ditches?" Though she wasn't precisely sure of the function of ditches. Drainage, sure, but they must have other purposes. Capable as he was, Sammy would know. Maybe she'd ask him if she ever talked to him again.

"I can't talk to you when you're like this."

That's a relief, Mother. I don't want to be talked to.

"So?" Leslie asked. "Where are we on this?"

Pam's legs itched from the heat and the wool of the settee. Her stomach growled from the lack of food since lunch yesterday. At least she wasn't horny anymore.

"Where are we on what?"

"This ... this whatever you've got going on with this Sammy person."

"Don't worry about it, Mother. Just don't. Sammy is only in town until after the concert."

"But what about the concert?"

"What about it?"

"You are being purposefully obtuse. What about your date?"

"My what?"

"Miller!"

"Miller! Miller who?" She had no idea what her mother was talking about, and she was getting really tired of this. "The miller from *Rumpelstiltskin*? Or the one from the *The Canterbury Tales*? Miller Genuine Draft?"

"Stop pretending, Pam. Miller—Angie's brother. You do remember Angie, don't you? Your sister-in-law?"

Then it all came back to her, though evidently not the way her mother remembered.

"I told you no. I told you I would be too busy. I don't have a date that night with Miller or Sammy or Rumpelstiltskin or anyone else. I have a job to do. So if this ... the fabulous *Miller* is expecting me to dance attention on him, then you had better disabuse him of the notion." She stood up. She'd had enough. Too much. "You know what? I think I'll go stay with Audrey downtown until after the concert is over. That'll give you more room for Kurt and Angie and whoever else they might bring along." Audrey lived in the apartment above Heavenly Confections. She'd be glad to have her and it was a fair bet she had working air conditioning. "I'm going to pack a bag right now."

Her mother stood up from the piano bench. "Pam, come back here."

But Pam didn't. She stalked off to the sound of Leslie's hands crashing on the keyboard, twice as loud and twice as furious as before.

CHAPTER 13

Having installed herself at Audrey's, Pam was in better shape by the time she got to work—or at least she was showered, cool, and fed.

Now, if she could just not think—not think about Sammy, not think about how this week was going to play out, and—above all else—not think about the things her mother had said. It wasn't that she agreed with Leslie's opinion about Sammy, but it did unearth a little germ of a thought that had drifted through her brain a few times.

The fact was the Beaufords didn't treat him well. How dare Gabe forget to do what he'd promised to do with no regard for Sammy? And how dare Jackson demand that Sammy drive to Tennessee on short notice, so late at night? Okay, not *that* late, but still.

And she could easily see that Sammy felt there was no way he could tell them no. That was no life—especially for someone with the kind of skills Sammy had. All Sammy lacked was confidence.

Not that any of this was going to matter. There was no way to avoid contact with him. They still had a concert to put on. But they were over. She could fool herself into thinking otherwise, but that wouldn't make it true. Even if he had meant that romantic talk about wanting to see her coming toward him with lace on her head, long distance relationships didn't stand much of a chance, especially since she had a job she couldn't leave, and he had one he would cut his arm off before leaving. Probably for the best. There were too many Beaufords to play second fiddle to now, and they were bound to breed more.

Thankfully, Lucy gave her a stack of special orders to place—not creative and fun, but not mindless either. Best of all, it would take hours and she could hide in the back at her desk to do it.

She worked steadily until Lucy approached her desk.

"Almost done," Pam said. "Low Country Design's website is down, but I was about to call."

"It can wait. Probably best to wait until after lunchtime anyway."

"Is it that late?" Pam looked at her computer. It *was* that late. And they never made calls to suppliers between noon and two, when there was likely to be a skeleton staff.

Lucy smiled. "It's after twelve. You have a visitor."

And there was no doubt who it would be. Though she hadn't realized she'd been expecting him, she wasn't even surprised. She stood up. Might as well get it done.

"Thank you, Lucy. I'll just take my lunch."

As Pam walked away, Lucy spoke again. "Pam? Take all the time you need. I'll call Low Country."

Sammy stood near the front of the store, looking out the side window so that she saw him in profile. He didn't see her at first. Instead of his familiar faded jeans or knee-length athletic shorts and T-shirt, today he wore khaki shorts, a white polo shirt, and topsiders that had seen better days. Her mother would have approved of this look—especially the worn shoes. She said men should look like they had things, not that they had bought things.

Though she'd made no noise and little movement, he turned and looked at her as though he could sense her presence. His smile was tentative but sweet. He looked tired.

"Hi." He lightly touched her arm when she stepped close enough. "I told you I could have had you back by noon."

"Was your trip okay?"

He nodded. "Fine. Not so fine as if you had been with me, but fine enough."

"Good."

He looked around. "Can we go somewhere? Maybe get some lunch? Are you hungry? I have some things to say to you."

Since he'd experienced the rough side of her tongue, it was a sure bet that he was going to tell her this had all been a mistake and, regardless of her confusion and uncertainty, she was probably going to cry. That couldn't happen at the diner.

"We don't have air conditioning at my house right now, so I'm staying with Audrey for a while. We can go there." No need to tell him the whole story.

"No AC?" He took her arm and ushered her out the door. "That's rough."

"Lightning struck."

"It sure did." His voice was heavy and reflective. There was no doubt what he meant. She hoped he knew she wasn't expecting sex. She hoped she wasn't.

"You look nice," Pam said, though to tell the truth, she missed the faded T-shirt and Converse.

"I can clean up when I need to. I thought I might need all the help I could get today."

Nothing to say to that, so they walked up the block in silence.

"I have a key," Pam said as they neared Heavenly Confections. "We can go down the alley and in the back door."

She was in no mood to pass the time of day with whoever had stopped by the shop at lunchtime for coffee and a sweet treat. Finally, something went right. They managed to make it up the stairs and into Audrey's sparse, neat apartment without running into anyone.

They stood in the middle of the living room, and Sammy looked around. "Nice."

"No one ever lives here long. First Lanie, then Arabelle, now Audrey. They all got engaged while living here."

"Yeah? Then I'm glad you're living here."

Her stomach rolled. "Sammy, don't tease me."

He took her hand. "Can we sit down?"

She let him lead her to the sofa, where they sat down together. All of a sudden, she didn't think she could stand to hear what he had to say. Better to say it herself. Not only had the china teacup shattered, she couldn't even find the pieces.

"Look," she said. "You don't need to say anything. It was fun. I knew the risk—someone like you and someone like me. We don't belong together. You can do better." She looked at her hands.

"What are you talking about? Pam, stop looking at your hands and look at me. Explain what you mean."

He looked genuinely confused.

She took a deep breath. She'd started it so she had to finish it.

"You have an exciting life with those Beaufords. I pick out paint chips. Everybody likes you. I'm subdued. After leaving college, I didn't have a single close friend until Audrey came along. My parents don't even like me. I didn't do anything like they expected. They're ashamed that I didn't finish college or have a professional career. Plus, there's the way you look. You've got to know how exceptional you are.

You've looked in the mirror. And I'm ordinary—less than ordinary. You're out of my league."

He shook his head. "First of all, shame on your parents if that's how they really feel. You are fine, good, and smart. If they don't see that, then it's their loss. I'm not saying anything else about that, because they're your parents and I haven't the right. But as for that other stuff—I have plenty of right to have my say about that. *I'm* out of *your* league? You don't even know how crazy that is. It's exactly what I thought the first time I saw you. Why do you think I mooned over you for three months but didn't try to get in contact with you?"

"You don't have to say that."

"Yes, I do." He took her by the shoulders. "Listen to me. I know this has been fast, but it doesn't feel like it to me. I told you I loved you last night, and I meant it. You could do better. I know it. But I think you have feelings for me. Deny it if you can," he challenged.

She dropped her eyes. "No. I can't deny it."

"That's what I thought. And I'm going to have you if you're fool enough to have me."

She opened her mouth to say, what, she didn't know.

"No, Pam. Let me speak. I've thought this out. I ran it all through my head while I was on the road, and then I did some exploring on the Internet."

"The Internet? The Beaufords can't look up woodworking on the Internet, just have to have a book. But you're researching relationships?"

"Of course not. Hear me out. First off, I didn't like being away from you. I didn't like it worth a damn. I wanted you with me, in my bed, in my life. I want you to meet my parents and my sister. I want you to know the Beaufords. So I want you to move back to Beauford Bend with me when I go."

He could have asked her to migrate to Mars on the back of a flying orangutan and she wouldn't have been any more surprised.

"Move to Beauford Bend? Right after the concert is over? And live with you and those Beaufords? Just like that?"

"More or less. It would be preferable for you to go back when I do, but I can see where you might have to give a couple of weeks' notice. And you wouldn't be living with the Beaufords. Just me. My little house only has five rooms. But it's nice. And bigger than this place." He gestured to the apartment.

"Sammy, it's not a question of space …"

"I don't expect you to just live with me." He took her hand and looked into her eyes. "I want to marry you. Hell, I'd marry you today. But I know women need time to get all that together—the dress, flowers, shoes, and all."

There was no doubt. The circus was in town and she was a member of it. Her brain was a kaleidoscope. *Love. Moving to Beauford Bend. Marriage?* When they were supposed to be breaking up.

"Sammy, I have a job, a job I like. No one else would let me do what Annelle and Lucy do. I told you that."

He looked really excited at that. "That's what I read up on. You don't have to work for someone else. You can have your own business."

Not him, too. "Sammy, I told you. I am not a good student. I don't even want to go back to school."

"And I don't want you to. You don't have to."

What the hell? "I thought you read up on this."

"I did. And I know you can't tell people you are an interior designer. I get that. But you can open a decorating store of your own, just like Miss Annelle's. So long as you don't say you're a designer, there's nothing stopping you from helping people pick their colors and furniture. You can call yourself a decorator all day long. People won't care. And there's nothing like that in Beauford unless you count the Sherwin-Williams paint store."

"It's not that simple. First off, you're talking about a huge financial undertaking. I don't have any money to speak off. Do you know how much it would take to open a shop like that?"

"As a matter of fact, I do."

"Let me guess. You looked it up on the Internet."

"No. I didn't know enough about it to figure it out. Gabe did."

"Gabe? *Gabe Beauford?* Gabe, who was supposed to take care of that book business but didn't?"

"That's right. He owed me, so I called and woke him up. He cussed at me, but he did what I wanted—even got excited about it. He's scattered, but he's a good guy and a good businessman. He handles his own investments and runs the business side of Rafe's rough stock business."

"Rafe's what?" It was getting hard to breathe. With every word Sammy spoke, the terror grew. It was as though he were stacking bricks on her chest.

"He breeds rodeo animals. But none of that matters. You can do this. As for money, I have some. I don't really have any expenses. I earn good money and get a lot of bonuses. Gabe has helped me invest. And here's the best part, Pam. Gabe said he and Neyland would invest in a decorator shop for you. Neyland bought a building for her jewelry business downtown. It's way too big, so you could move right in. Jackson thinks it's a great idea."

"Jackson does, does he? And you and Gabe figured all this out." Fear was replaced little by little with anger.

He nodded. "Fast, huh? Slow never got me a damned thing."

She closed her eyes and rubbed the place between them.

"So I'm supposed to sell myself to the Beaufords, like you have."

His smile froze and faded. "What do you mean? I work for Jackson, just like you work for Annelle and Lucy."

"Annelle and Lucy don't call me on a whim for a ridiculous errand. They value me. The Beaufords don't value you."

The hurt in his eyes killed a little piece of her soul—just as her words must have killed a little piece of his.

"And that's what you think that was last night? Ridiculous? Well, it wasn't. Beau had a hard time making a life for himself after he got hurt in the military. But he has, and Will Garrett is a hard man to please. Will said get the book, and he had to have the book."

"Then he should have come and gotten it himself."

Sammy put his hands up. "No. We aren't talking about the particulars. It's none of your business, and it's none of mine. It's my job to make their lives easier, and I am paid well for it. And it isn't even about the money. They were good to me when I was young, dumb, with no skills. They treat me like family." He closed his eyes briefly. "As for the Beaufords not valuing me—if you think I'm worthless to them as a person, it sounds like you're the one who doesn't value me."

That cut into her gut like she had swallowed glass shards.

"I'm sorry I said that. I didn't mean it quite like that. I just meant they could be more considerate of you."

"Maybe it does seem like they don't consider me, but that's their way. It's how they treat each other. But when it matters, they are there. Once when I was on the road with Jackson, I fell off the stage and got a concussion. He had plenty of people he could have had take care of me, but he sat up with me all night himself and woke me every two hours. And then he did his show the next day after having almost no sleep. Another time, when Jackson and Emory were going out of town, I was supposed to take care of

Beauford Bend, only my sister broke her arm while her husband was at army reserve camp. Gabe changed his plans and stayed so I could go to Birmingham and take care of Sonja and her baby. And I could name you a hundred more times when they took care of me just like I take care of them."

"All right. I admit I don't know enough about your relationship to judge, and I shouldn't have. But I do know how capable you are. You could do more than be at their beck and call. You could have people working for *you*. You don't even realize how competent you are, how you think of everything. I've told you before you could do anything. And you should."

He sat for minute and digested that. "You know what I think? I think you want me to be just what your parents want you to be—something I'm not."

"Didn't you just ask that of me with this harebrained decorating shop idea?"

"No, Pam. The difference is you said you *couldn't* do anything else other than what you're doing. I said I didn't *want* to."

"But you could ..."

"Could what? Work at something that would be more acceptable to you? To your parents? You keep saying I can do anything, but you don't even have a concrete idea about what that anything is. You just want me to do something better. Which is it, Pam? Am I too good for you? Or not good enough for you? I can dissuade you of one and accept the other, but I don't know what to do with both."

Shame crept through her. "I didn't mean it like that. I could never think you weren't good enough for me. I just want the best for you—because I do value you. You don't even know how much."

He nodded. "Well. That's good to hear anyway. But I have the best. Or I would if I can have you, too. Can I?"

A big part of her wanted to say yes, but it was going to have to be his way if it was to be.

"I don't know. You're asking a lot of me."

He nodded. "People generally do ask a lot of the people they love with all their hearts—sooner or later. For me, it's just sooner."

"I can't give you an answer right now. I don't even know if I can run a shop."

He shrugged. "I know you can if that's what you want, but you don't have to. You can get a different job—maybe for one of those artisans in town. Or you can cook and have some babies. I don't care so long as you're happy."

She had to laugh a little at that. "You seem sure I can cook."

"Can you? Not that you have to. I can."

"So can I," she said. "Well enough."

"Do you ever wear an apron?" He was as close to looking happy as he had today.

"No. This isn't the first time you've brought up aprons. What's with that?"

"Just a fantasy I have. Are we ever going to have a fantasy, Pam?" He didn't wait for an answer. "I accept that you can't give me an answer. I understand this is your whole life. But can you do one thing?"

"What is it?"

"Can you admit that you love me?"

She had hurt him today. She could at least give him the truth about this. "Yes. I can do that. As you said, it was fast. Audrey says when you know, you know. And she's right. I do love you. There's just a lot to consider."

This should have been a joyful moment that ended with kisses and promises, but it wasn't, because she still couldn't quite believe he loved her.

They leaned their foreheads together. "Then I believe we can find our way," Sammy said.

"I hope so." And that was true.

He sat up abruptly and spread his hands. "Look. We've got a concert to put on. We've got a lot to think about, mull over. Let's just let this go for now, let it lie. We can talk about it after the concert."

She knew the relief that set in would be short-lived, but she embraced it all the same.

"So, can we get some lunch?" Sammy asked. "I need to bring you up to speed on how we're going to handle Jackson's personal security."

And he took her hand, but he didn't try to kiss her.

CHAPTER 14

Sammy had had some long weeks in his life, but none like this. Thank God it was nearly over. The concert was tomorrow night. Jackson and company had hit town today, and there was a pool party going on not twenty feet from where Sammy sat in the dark pool house.

He missed Pam. It wasn't that he hadn't seen her. After all, they had concert details to attend to—not many, but it gave him a chance to see her every day. But there was a void.

He had to keep his promise to not press her until the concert was over. People were always talking about "giving somebody space," which he'd always taken to mean, "I'm outta here." Maybe that's what it meant this time, but he didn't know what else to do. He had managed to keep his hands and mouth off of her. And that was hard.

But this time tomorrow night, he'd have an answer.

There was a knock on the door, and he practically flew there. Maybe Pam had come after all.

He'd asked her to come tonight, but she'd declined—said she had to have dinner with her family because her brother had just flown in. He couldn't help but notice that he'd wanted her to meet the Beauford clan, but she hadn't asked him to meet her family.

He should have known it wouldn't be her at the door. It was only Jackson and Gabe.

"So this is where you disappeared to," Jackson said.

Sammy stepped aside to let them enter. "What? No Rafe and Dirk?" Beau hadn't come. He was home building a birdhouse or something.

"We're glad to see you, too," Gabe said.

"Rafe and Dirk are putting kids to bed." Jackson handed him an open beer and started turning on lights. "What are you doing in here in the dark? Did you even eat?"

"I wasn't hungry."

Gabe took the best chair. "That's woman trouble if I've ever seen it."

"You've seen it." Jackson took the end of the couch where Sammy usually sat. "You've seen it in the mirror."

"I told you to get her a churn," Gabe said. "Did you tell her our plan?"

Sammy sat and took a drink of his beer. "Blasted it at her like red spray paint on a water tower. She's thinking."

Jackson and Gabe groaned. "Never good," Jackson said.

"This is my fault," Gabe said.

"Yeah. It really is," Sammy said. "Everything was going just fine. The trouble started when Jackson called me to get that damned book—which would not have happened if you'd done what you were supposed to in the first place."

"Will you let that go?" Gabe said. "I forgot! Sue me! Anyway that wasn't what I meant. I meant I've been too busy with the football camp to talk to you. I could have advised you. But it's over now, so I'm all yours."

"No, thanks. I've got this," Sammy said.

"Clearly," Jackson said. "It does sound unreasonable that

she got mad over that. Maybe she's not the one for you. Call her up and get her over here. I want to look her over."

"No," Sammy said. "You're not looking anybody over. She *is* the one for me. And it wasn't so much that she got mad that I had to take the book to Beau—at least I don't think it was that. Let's just say that the call came at an inopportune time."

Gabe and Jackson exchanged glances.

"You mean to tell me," Gabe said slowly, "that you answered the phone when you were having sex?" Gabe broke into gales of laughter, and if that wasn't bad enough, Jackson joined in.

"You sound like eighth grade girls. Stop it. Especially you." Sammy looked at Jackson. "I didn't have a choice. You called me on the right-damn-now phone."

"Sammy, there is always a choice. Don't answer the phone during sex, even for me—especially for me. Call me back, preferably after you've bathed."

"That's what you say now. If I did that, you'd want to know where the hell I'd been."

"I wouldn't." Jackson shook his head laughing. "If you didn't answer, I'd know where the hell you'd been. Maybe I ought to get a right-damn-now-even-if-you're-having-sex phone, though I can't think of anything that would call for that. Even if somebody dies, they'll still be dead when you're done."

Sammy sighed. "No. It's my fault. I don't know how to talk to her. I live to anticipate and fix. I'm good at it."

"The best," Jackson agreed.

"But where she's concerned, I don't know whether to shit or go blind. Hell. I'd consult a Ouija board if I had one—and I am here to tell you that's something that was frowned on by the Bethel Baptist Church youth group. They schooled me to steer clear of it regardless of the circumstances."

"Welcome aboard, brother," Jackson said. "We've all been there and lived to tell it. You will, too."

He hoped so.

"You know," Gabe said. "I've always wondered what situation exists that could possibly be helped by shitting or going blind."

CHAPTER 15

Pam drove toward the Avery farm with her car weighted down by the cases of Gatorade that Big Starr market had given her for the football players who were serving the barbecue tonight.

Tonight was the night, and Pam was excited—happy excited for the first time in a while.

It had been a long, hard, busy week firming up commitments for the concert, running from her mother, and finishing Sophie Ann's hideous bedroom.

But the hardest part had been seeing Sammy and feeling the distance between them. He was only doing what they'd promised, but every time she'd seen him and he hadn't tried to touch her, it had broken her heart.

But that was over. After all the angst and fear that she couldn't make a go of the decorating shop or the relationship, it had come to her that she had to try. She had to try because she wanted both—her own shop and Sammy —badly.

She laughed a little to herself. *Come to her,* indeed. That sounded like a fairy had sprinkled magic dust in her ear while she slept, when it had really come in the form of tough love from Audrey.

Between helping with the camp and spending as much time with her fiancé as she could manage, Audrey had not spent a lot time at the apartment where Pam was still staying. What time they had been together, Pam had done a fair share of moaning, and Audrey had done a lot of hand patting.

But last night, Audrey had come in from the last day of camp hot, hungry, and eager to get to Missy's pool party, where Max was already visiting with his cousins.

"Great," Audrey said when she saw that Pam was dressed to go out. "You changed your mind about the pool party. I'm glad."

"Hardly." Pam had come to hate the sigh in her voice. "My brother flew in. I'm going to dinner at the club with the family."

"You should go the party." Audrey had been saying that ever since Sammy had invited her. "You can see your brother tomorrow."

"I don't know …"

Pam expected a soft word from her friend, but Audrey rounded on her, ponytail flying, and put her hands in the air.

"For God's sake, Pam! Stop it. I swear, if you say 'I don't know' one more time— Just stop the whining. I love you. I do. And I've tried to act like a romantic comedy movie friend would, but I can't listen to this anymore. You keep talking about the china teacup shattering. I don't even know what you're talking about. There is no damned teacup. There's you and Sammy, and you've wanted him ever since last March when he came in Annelle's shop to pick up that rug. And he wants you. Just tell him yes."

"But my job—"

"Open your own damned shop. You want to. So what if you're not an interior designer? So what if a big, fancy hotel chain isn't going to hire you? You don't want to do that anyway. You just want to help people put their homes together. You're good at it and you won't fail. But if you do, if you lose your investors' money, Sammy loves you anyway, and Gabe Beauford can afford it. Just stop saying, 'I don't know.' I can't take any more of this, even if you can."

Pam had felt like ice water had been poured on her head.

Audrey had clapped a hand over her mouth. "I'm sorry."

Pam had waited for the hurt and mad to set in, but it didn't. "No. No. I'm sorry."

Audrey had shaken her head. "I don't want you to be sorry. I want you to be happy."

"What if I go and it goes wrong?"

Audrey had shrugged. "Then you'll come home no worse off than when you left."

"But it would hurt to have him and lose him."

"Will it hurt if you lose him because you tell him no?"

And that had been the defining moment.

To hell with the china teacup.

She wouldn't leave with him on Sunday. Annelle and Lucy deserved notice and to hear what she was planning, though she was sure they would be supportive.

But she was going to tell him tonight as soon as the concert was over and, after that, she was going to see to it that he put his hands on her.

On second thought, she wasn't going to wait until after the concert. She was going to tell him as soon as she could steal a minute. Then they'd have the rest of the night to anticipate the after.

CHAPTER 16

People were arriving in droves, and Sammy was in his element. The weather was nice, nobody was drunk, Jackson was pleased with the stage, and everything was in order for the VIP section. He regretted giving those passes to Pam's mother. How dare those people make her feel like a failure? He'd see to it that she showed them—if she would just say the right thing.

And somehow, he thought she would. He hadn't talked to her, but there she was now organizing the caterers. He caught her eye, and she smiled a smile so bright and sunny that it turned his heart to mush. And there was the proof that she was going to tell him what he wanted to hear. It was only in that moment that he realized how shrouded she had been with gloom and misery. But it was gone, and he was going to make it his life's work to see that she never looked that unhappy again.

Too soon, she disappeared into the barn with a little wave. He went backstage and checked to make sure that Jackson's guitars were set up in the order that he would need them. The guitar techs never got it wrong, but Sammy liked to make sure.

He fully intended to go to the VIP section and get a look at Pam's mother's and sister-in-law's engagement rings. He was going commission a ring from Neyland Beauford for Pam that made theirs look like Cracker Jack prizes. It meant something to have a Neyland Beauford original. He might not be rich like the Beaufords—or rich at all—but he could afford that. Besides, Neyland worked for cost for family, and he was family.

"Sammy." Jackson's manager's voice came through his headset.

"Yeah, Ginger?"

"Jackson's ready for you." That meant it was time to wire him for the show and give him a weather and attendance report while he ate a Clif bar and drank two bottles of water.

Before heading to Jackson's trailer, Sammy cast his eyes around for another look at Pam. He didn't see her, but that was okay.

Pretty soon, he'd see her every morning.

A half hour later, Sammy took Jackson's empty water bottles and Clif bar wrapper. "Are you hydrated enough? It's hot."

"If I hydrate any more, I won't get through the first number without peeing."

"All right then." Sammy picked up two towels and five T-shirts that were identical to the one Jackson wore. He would sweat through at least three before the night was over. "I'm going to make sure your cooler has plenty of water. I'll see you in the wings."

"Sammy," Jackson called.

"Yeah? You need something else?"

"Don't wait for me in the wings tonight. Just leave the cooler and my towels and clean shirts. Go get your girl."

"You sure?" It was almost time for the show to start, which meant Pam ought be finished overseeing the food being served.

Jackson laughed. "Believe it or not, there was a time when people didn't wait on me hand and foot."

With that on his mind, Sammy left the trailer and stumbled right into the arms of a woman—but not the right woman.

"Sammy! I was waiting for you!" She pulled his mouth down to meet hers with such force that his hands flew to her shoulders to steady them both. She smelled wrong, her shoulders were too bony, and her mouth tasted wrong.

It took some force to disengage, but he managed. He looked at the face before him and searched his brain for a name. She was one of the concert followers—one he'd slept with once. Or was it twice? He should have expected this, even with the tickets so scarce, because groupies seemed to always find a way.

"Ursula." He couldn't find her last name, wasn't sure he'd ever known it.

"I drove nineteen hours to get here just to see you!"

"Uh, right." He was more than sure she hadn't thought about him any more than he had thought about her.

And that's when he saw her—Pam. She stood not five feet from them with wide eyes. Her hand flew to cover her mouth.

"Pam!"

She put up a hand as if to ward him off and turned and ran.

"Uh oh. Looks like Sammy's in trouble," Ursula trilled.

"Get out of my way, Ursula." But he didn't wait. He shoved his way around her, dropped Jackson's towels and shirts, and started to run.

~

*P*am climbed the ladder to the barn loft. This was the last place she wanted to go, so she figured it was the last place Sammy would look for her—if he looked for her at all.

How could she possibly have been so stupid? How could she have thought plain old Pam could have something that exotic, tall, blond Ursulas were out there wanting?

It was hot in the loft, but she wouldn't be here long. She just needed a place to hide for a bit until she could compose herself. If it were possible, she would leave, but she was in charge of this event, and there were still a hundred things that could go wrong—fire, flood, overflowing portable toilets, flooding because of the overflowing portable toilets.

The mattress was still up here, but she refused to look at it, let alone sit on it. She walked over to the large open window to catch a breeze and watch for floods.

"Pam."

Damn it all to hell. She turned. "What are you doing here?"

"Looking for you. I figured this was the last place you'd want to go, so I looked here first."

So much for that.

"You were looking for me," he said. There was not a question in his voice.

No point in denying it, but she could save face. "I was. Since I'd made my decision, I didn't see the point of waiting until the concert was over. I thought I'd go ahead tell you that things can't work out between us."

"You're lying." He moved until he stood in front of her. "That's not what you came to tell me. You came to tell me we were going to live happily ever after."

Again, no point in denying it. She didn't have the energy.

"Yeah, well." She picked at her cuticles. "That was then. This is—as you say—right damn now."

"Pam, that wasn't what it looked like."

"Oh please, Sammy. Spare me the cliché. I can't even fathom how many millions of men have said that to an equal number of women."

"I'm not one of those men. I'm the one who's in love with you and only wants you. She's one of a whole group of women who follow Jackson on the road. She surprised me."

"Oh, she did? *Ursula* surprised you?"

"That's right. I stepped out of Jackson's trailer with nothing on my mind but finding you. The next thing I knew, she was kissing me, but I did not kiss her back."

"Is that like smoking pot but not inhaling?"

"I don't know anything about that. I don't do drugs and Ouija boards. Or kiss women other than you. Not anymore."

Ouija boards? She almost let that distract her. "She didn't have any trouble believing it would be all right to kiss you. I don't go around assuming that random men would be okay with me kissing them. So I'm guessing you've kissed her before. And slept with her."

"Well…" The story was on his face. "Not recently."

"Really? How recent?"

"I don't know. A while back. A year. Nine months. I don't really remember much about it. They all run together."

All. Well, great. "They do, do they? So I guess I'm just somebody to run together with the rest of them. Do you stockpile those lace shawls?"

His face went from red to white and back to red. "That's not fair. I have never invited another woman to Beauford Bend—"

"The sacred, the *holy* Beauford Bend!" Her voice was louder than she intended.

"Much less asked anyone to move in with me, to *marry* me." He raised his voice to overtake hers.

They stopped and glared at each other.

"Look." Sammy spread his hands, palms up. "Please, let's not fight. What you saw was a misunderstanding. I did not know she was coming. I did not participate in the kiss, and I got away from her and came after you. I want you. I knew we were feeling the same thing when we saw each other earlier, before you went in the barn with the barbecue people."

She knew that moment, had felt it, too. It felt like forever ago. She bit her lip to keep the tears from spilling.

"Don't let one stupid moment destroy us, Pam. It was nothing."

It would be easy to tell him she believed him, but it would be a lie.

"There is no us, Sammy. I'm just glad I found it out before I quit my job and moved in with you, or—God forbid, married you."

He nodded. "Yeah," he said softly. "God forbid. God forbid that you might take a chance to be happy."

That was so not fair. "I was going to take a chance. I was ready. But then—"

"But then, nothing," he interrupted. "Nothing happened. You're looking for an excuse. You were looking for an excuse not to be with me when I was too good for you—or was it not good enough? It changed minute to minute. And I talked you down. You know why? Because I love you and you're worth everything to me. But I'm not going to try to talk you down again. I have never lied to you. You may be out of my league, like I have always thought, but I've done nothing to deserve this."

"I don't need an excuse, Sammy. It's not like I'm trying to get out of gym class or jury duty."

"That's right. I'm asking you one more time not to do this

to us, to give us a chance. Let this be a misunderstanding that we laugh about with our grandchildren."

If only that were possible. "I can't."

"Okay. I've begged enough. I'm done with it. But know this, Pam. If I walk away from you, I won't come back."

"That's for the best." She couldn't even feel her heart anymore.

He stood and looked at her for a long minute. "From the first, you were like music in my head. Just music. I'm not musical, so I didn't have a song. But now I do. It's an old Frankie Valli song. 'Walk Like a Man.' And that's what I'm going to do."

And he did. She watched him go, and then she watched out the window. She waited until she saw him walking back toward the stage with his head held high before she let herself cry.

CHAPTER 17

Pam was in the shop alone and grateful for it.

The camp and concert that had taken over her life for months and the whole town for a week, was now four days gone. Except for a very fat check for the arts center, it was like it never happened. Well, that and her sore heart.

She knew Sammy was staying through the weekend, when the stage would be broken down, so Pam waited until yesterday—Monday—to go out to the Avery property to make sure everything had been left in good order. But it was a formality. She knew Sammy wouldn't leave on Sunday until everything was perfect, because that's the kind of man he was.

Luke had been complimentary. "If anything, it's cleaner than it was before the concert. But there is one thing. There was a mattress in the loft. Do you know anything about that?"

"No idea," she'd lied. It was unlike Sammy to forget something like that. Maybe he hadn't. Maybe he couldn't stand to look at it either.

Luke had just laughed and said it didn't matter, but they'd

have to get rid of it before it was time for the kids to build their homecoming float. Pam had joined in the laughter, but it was manufactured, like everything else about her these days.

She had moved back into her parents' house, and things were calm for the moment—or maybe not so much calm as flat. Everything felt flat, dusty, and used up.

Especially her. And it was quiet. Maybe people knew she was grieving and were keeping their distance. Or maybe they were just living their lives without any thought to her. Either way, mercifully, no one had tried to talk to her about it except Audrey.

But she didn't want to talk about it to Audrey, or anyone else, didn't want to explore the possibility that she might have been wrong. Not that it mattered. He'd said if he walked away, he wouldn't come back. If he was nothing else, Sammy was a man of his word.

Sammy was a man of his word. That was something she didn't want to think about.

And luckily for her, the door swung open and in walked a distraction in the form of Missy Bragg.

"Pam! How are you? Recovered yet?"

"Mostly." She would never recover. "How about you?"

"Mostly. I loved having a houseful of people, but it's good to get back to normal, too."

"You did a great job," Pam said. "Nobody could have done better."

"Thank you." Missy didn't even bother to act humble. "You did a great job, too. The concert and barbecue were perfect and almost pure profit. I hope we can do it again next year, and I hope you'll be in charge again."

"We'll see." That would never happen, but it wouldn't matter. Anyone could fill her shoes, because the success had all been Sammy's. "Did you need some help with something?"

"Not really. I need a little bread-and-butter hostess gift. I'll just look around until I see something I like."

"If I can help you, let me know."

"You can help *me!*" Just when the day couldn't get any worse. Pam had not heard Sophie Ann come in, and she was clearly furious.

Missy even looked a little scared and walked over to explore a display of scented candles.

"You know I'm always happy to help you, Mrs. McGowan." Sophie Ann had instructed Pam a while back to use her given name, but that wasn't going to fly today. "How was your trip?"

"My trip was wonderful until it was ruined by what I came home to last night."

She had forgotten Sophie Ann was due back yesterday. "Was something amiss? I inspected everything after the workman finished to be sure there was no mess."

"Then why did you leave things as they were? It's horrible! I've never seen anything like it. It wasn't what I had in mind at all."

So exactly what Pam had feared was happening. Oddly, she didn't care all that much.

"I was afraid of that." Pam went behind the counter, pulled Sophie Ann's file, and spread the paint chips and swatches on the counter—the very ones that she'd thrown in the air when Sammy startled her and he had gathered up so carefully. "The colors are very bold. That's why I suggested more muted tones and mixing in some browns and greens."

Sophie Ann waved her silent. "I am not interested in how you created this mess. I want to know what's going to be done to fix it."

"I could come out and make some suggestions," Pam said.

"I don't think so. Where are Annelle and Lucy?"

"Out on separate consultation visits. They'll be back in

later."

"Send them out as soon as possible. Both of them. And tell Annelle Mead I'm not paying a penny until this is rectified."

And with that, Sophie Ann slammed out the door.

This would have sent Pam to the back in tears a short time ago, but she just shrugged and laid Sophie Ann's file aside. Annelle and Lucy would need it "as soon as possible."

"Good riddance." Missy stepped up to the counter. "Don't let it worry you."

"I won't. I tried to tell her. The room looks like a Halloween carnival clown. But she wouldn't have it any other way."

Missy laughed. "She had it coming. When we were fifteen, Brantley and I drank a whole bottle of Thunderbird, and she told on us. I never did find out how she knew it."

"I'm glad you got your pound of flesh."

"I don't understand why people don't listen. I heard you say you tried to tell her."

"Perception," Pam said. "She had this idea in her mind that she wanted her bedroom to look like autumn leaves. She had a preconceived notion of how it would look and would not be dissuaded, no matter what the truth was. Perception and truth can be very different."

Suddenly, Pam went cold.

No matter what the truth was. Preconceived notion. Sammy was a man of his word.

Pam could almost feel the color drain from her face. She gripped the counter to keep her knees from buckling.

Missy studied her and smiled a little knowing smile. "We all do that sometimes, Pam. Don't we?"

Pam nodded. "I have made a very bad mistake." She hadn't meant to say that out loud. What they had wasn't a china teacup at all. It was a solid gold chalice. Or it had been. It was as lost as the Holy Grail.

Missy nodded again. "Go get him."

Clearly she had no secrets. "I can't. He said if I sent him away, he wouldn't come back."

"Don't ask him to. *You* go to *him*."

"Isn't it the same thing? Besides, I … I can't. Not after all that."

Missy slammed her hand on the counter. "Don't you dare stand there and tell me you can't! I won't hear it. You go pack a bag this instant and go to Beauford Bend. Do it."

"What if he's not there?"

"He's there. Stop wasting time—mine and yours. Do what I tell you."

"You're sure he's there?"

Missy just rolled her eyes. Of course she knew.

Partially from fear of Missy Bragg, but mostly because of a small seed of hope, Pam moved toward the door—then stopped.

"I can't leave! Annelle and Lucy—"

"Get your ass out of here." Missy pointed to the door. "I'll stay here until they get back."

"What if—"

Missy pointed to the door again. "You have said *what if* too many times already."

Pam was almost out the door, when she suddenly turned back and plucked a natural-colored, French linen apron from a kitchen display.

"Tell Annelle I'll pay for this."

"I'll pay for it." Missy waved her off. Maybe she knew Sammy's fantasy, too—whatever it was.

Pam hesitated for a second. "You don't need a hostess gift, do you?"

"Of course, I do." Missy grinned. "Which is not to say I wasn't multitasking."

CHAPTER 18

Sammy had taken up the most hated chore at Beauford Bend —replacing the fairy lights in the live oak trees that lined the road leading from the road to the house.

"You don't have to do that," Emory had told him. "We can get one of the part-time college kids to do it."

"I'm doing it," he said. "I don't think I'm too good."

"I never thought you did. At least wait until the sun goes down and it's not so hot."

But he hadn't waited. He'd even refused to use the cherry picker. He'd gone old school with a ladder and climbing the trees, because he wanted to be hot, dirty, and tired—most of all he wanted to be so tired that maybe, maybe he could sleep tonight.

This weekend was the memorial concert for the Beaufords' little sister that Jackson gave every year. It was a fancy affair at the Ryman—not fancy for him because he'd be working—but he'd envisioned Pam dressed up sitting with the Beauford wives. Now, he couldn't stand to think about it. With any luck, maybe he'd get heatstroke and die so he wouldn't have to go. He grunted a little at the drama of that.

If he thought it would do any good, he would break his vow and go chase her down—kidnap her if necessary. Too bad he wasn't a pirate. You couldn't get away from a pirate unless you were willing to get eaten by sharks or drown. And even he didn't think he was that bad.

But maybe she did. Anyway, he wasn't a pirate. He was a man with no job title and no wish for one—and he was the man without the woman he loved.

He worked steadily and quietly. He usually listened to music when doing tasks like this, but he couldn't—hadn't even brought his phone and earbuds. Every song was a love song.

He had just reached the top of a tree near the guard shack when he became aware of a woman yelling. Not really all that unusual. There were always fans and reporters up there, claiming to have business inside the gates. Good luck with that. It was probably easier to get into Fort Knox than Beauford Bend.

"Let me in and right damn now!" The hair on the back of his neck rose. That almost sounded like Pam. But he thought he saw her and heard her everywhere. He began to remove the old string of lights.

"I'm telling you, I'm not leaving here until I see him! I'll sleep on the grass if I have to." That wasn't unusual either. Everybody wanted to see Jackson, but Dirk ran a tight, tight ship. Not a pirate ship either—a lawful, Dirkified ship.

"Ma'am, please move along." That was Brett, the guard, speaking. Since Sammy could hear him, that meant he was out of the guardhouse, which meant they were just a step away from calling the police. But Sammy wasn't much interested. It happened at least once a week. Brett went on, "We've already tried to contact him. He isn't answering his phone, and he apparently doesn't have his headset. Now what that says to me is he doesn't want to see you." That didn't even make pretty good sense. The guards never, ever contacted Jackson. It was a rule—Dirk's rule, and nobody broke Dirk's rules. They might contact Dirk or Sammy to find out if maybe Jackson had failed to give them the name of someone he was expecting, but there was no contacting Jackson.

And then the woman started to cry. For some reason, Sammy's heart hurt a little at that. "But I've come all this way," she said. "All the way from Merritt."

He dropped the string of lights. Could it be? Afraid to look and afraid not to, he peered through the leaves.

They talked about miracles at the Bethel Baptist Church, but he was witnessing his own personal one. She had her back to him, but there was no doubt. It was Pam—and she'd been talking about him, not Jackson. He considered jumping out of the tree, but decided he needed to climb at least partway. When a man was offered a miracle, he didn't want to risk breaking his neck.

Finally on the ground, he moved as quickly as he could.

"Please," she begged. "Tell me. Have you ever been in love?"

Brett didn't answer her and seemed relieved when he caught sight of Sammy over Pam's shoulder.

"Let her in, Brett," Sammy said. "Open the gate."

Slowly, slowly like the molasses they loved, Pam turned and met his eyes. He held out his hand as the gate opened. When she walked toward him, he saw that she did not cry pretty. Her face was blotchy, her nose was running, and most of her mascara had repurposed itself into raccoon makeup.

He had never seen a more beautiful face.

When she reached him she said, "I know you said you wouldn't come back to me. And maybe you won't. But I hope you'll reconsider. And even if you don't, I need to tell you I made a very bad mistake. I will do—"

"Stop." She was close enough now for him to grasp her

arms. "Just stop. You had me at 'Let me in and right damn now.'"

Her expression froze as she processed words. And they began to laugh—and kiss.

He knew he'd never kiss another woman.

And from the way she kissed him back, he knew she knew it, too.

ABOUT THE AUTHOR

Jean Hovey is an emerging author of spy westerns. This is Jean's fourth book.

9 798884 340119